SHELTERED LOVE

By the Author

Shots Fired

Forbidden Passions

Initiation By Desire

Speakeasy

Escapades

Sheltered Love

SHELTERED LOVE

by

MJ Williamz

A Division of Bold Strokes Books

2015

SHELTERED LOVE

ISBN 13: 978-1-62639-362-2

This Trade Paperback Original Is Published By
Bold Strokes Books, Inc.
P.O. Box 249
Valley Falls, NY 12185

First Edition: July 2015

Credits
Editor: Cindy Cresap
Production Design: Stacia Seaman
Cover Design by Sheri (graphicartist2020@hotmail.com)

Acknowledgments

As always, my first thanks go to Laydin for everything she does for me, for her encouragement and support in the writing process. I'd also like to thank Sarah for believing in me and helping me get through this book, which was difficult to write at times. Also, a thank you to Speed for beta reading for me.

I'd also like to thank Cindy for editing my work for me and for Rad for still letting my books be published.

For Laydin—Forever

Chapter One

Boone Fairway stretched awake. Her arm bumped the woman next to her.

"Good morning, sleepy," the woman said.

"Good morning." Boone couldn't remember her bedmate's name.

"I need to get going." The woman climbed out of bed.

"Do you need a ride?" Boone asked.

"I drove last night, remember?"

"Oh, yeah." Boone rubbed her eyes as her head throbbed. She didn't remember much of the night before. She'd had way too many beers. But she commended herself on the nice-looking young woman getting dressed in front of her.

"So, Boone, you never told me. How old are you really?"

Boone kept her age a secret. Only her closest friends knew she was forty-two. She passed for a much younger woman and opted to let people assume she was.

"I don't talk about how old I am," she said.

"So you say. Usually only old people are that weird about their age. And you sure aren't old."

Boone looked at the woman staring at her. She was maybe in her mid-twenties. Boone wondered how old she thought "old people" were. She smiled.

"Thanks for last night," she said.

"My pleasure. I'll see you at the bar."

"I'll walk you out." Boone got out of bed and pulled on her boxers and undershirt. She walked the young woman to her door and kissed her before she opened the door for her.

With her company gone, Boone stepped in the shower and let the warm water wash away her hangover. She dried off and quickly donned cargo shorts and her Oregon T-shirt. The Ducks were playing that day, and she was ready for the bar to be packed.

She climbed into her black Nissan Frontier and drove to The Boonies, the bar she'd owned for almost twenty years. She walked in to find Christopher setting up the bar.

"You ready for a big day today?" she asked.

"We're going to be packed. It's the first game of the season. Go Ducks!"

"Go Ducks, indeed!"

Boone watched Christopher mopping around the four pool tables and lowering benches and stools. Boone turned on her televisions. There were three hours before the Ducks game, but there would be a few fans of SEC football coming in to watch their teams beforehand.

Soon the bar had a decent gathering of football fans. There were people watching the Georgia game and quite a few yelling "Roll Tide" as they watched Alabama. Boone was happy. She loved college football. She also loved that the season meant greater profit for the bar.

She jumped behind the bar to help her bartenders as more and more people came in to get warmed up for the Ducks game. They were playing some nobody team from the East Coast, but their loyal, die-hard fans were piling in to watch the blowout.

Just before kickoff, two more bartenders showed up, so Boone was able to relax on the other side of the bar and watch the game. As a U of O alumna, she was more than just another Oregonian who loved the blitz-like offense and fancy uniforms. She'd been a fan back when there wasn't a BCS and, even if there had been, the Ducks wouldn't have been contenders. No, she loved her Ducks passionately and was proud to have her bar be the go-to place for fans to watch the game.

She went behind the bar and grabbed a bottle of beer. The first sip tasted bitter, but she soon got past it and drank one after another as her beloved Ducks blew out their opponent. The game ended, and Boone invited a few of the patrons over to her place to swim and have a barbecue.

Boone grilled hamburgers and hot dogs for the twenty or so people who enjoyed her pool and hot tub. It wasn't unusual to party at Boone's place. She was known as a partier and womanizer. It wasn't that she was averse to the idea of a relationship. It was just that she hadn't met Ms. Right yet. She worked long hours and partied in her free time, so there wasn't really much time for her to meet someone to settle down with. While she had plenty of women sharing her bed, none of them were long-term material. And that worked for her.

As if on cue, one of the women climbed out of the hot tub and walked over to talk to Boone by the grill. The redhead's name was Dani, and she was a regular at the bar. They'd spent several nights together over the past couple of years.

"You work too hard. You should be in the water with us."

"I will after dinner," Boone said.

"Your Ducks looked amazing today."

"Yeah, they did. Must love the Ducks."

"Yeah, you do. Hey, would you like some company later on tonight?" Dani asked.

"I'd like that very much." Boone looked deep into Dani's dark green eyes.

"Good. I'll plan on staying here tonight."

❖

Grey Dawson lit the candles, grabbed her glass of white wine, and slipped into her bubble bath. She had the radio going in the background, the Oregon State Beavers game playing quietly. She wasn't a true football fan, but she followed her alma mater and liked the background noise of the game. She'd had a busy day at the local soup kitchen. She volunteered there every other Saturday. After her week at the shelter she managed and her day at the soup kitchen, she'd earned the bath. The bubbles, scented lavender vanilla, coated and soothed her.

She closed her eyes and reveled in the feeling. Soon, the combination of the wine and her team losing their home opener combined to make her melancholy. She considered the fact that she was home alone again on a Saturday night. She couldn't remember the last time she'd been on a date. She could count the times on one hand that she'd been out since she split up with Wynn, the abusive alcoholic she'd lived with for seven years.

She wondered briefly what she was doing wrong. She was attractive, intelligent, community-minded. She was also incredibly busy. The shelter she ran kept her busy for long hours every day. She knew she was married to her job. If she wanted to meet someone, she'd have to really put herself out there.

Grey was proud of the shelter she'd founded for victims of domestic abuse. She started the shelter five years ago, after almost fifteen years as a private practice counselor. There was a need in the community and she couldn't ignore it. Grey was always looking for ways to make her city a better place for all.

She got out of the tub and was toweling off when her phone rang. It was Cecilia from the shelter.

"Hello?"

"Grey, can you come down here? We've got a new intake, and she needs medical attention. I can't leave the shelter to take her."

"I'm on my way."

Grey pulled on a gray skirt and yellow blouse then slid into a pair of sandals, dressing quickly as she hurried to get out of the house. She wished, once again, that she had the funding for more staff at the shelter. Weekends were always the worst for new intakes, and she just didn't have the staff to accommodate all their needs.

She arrived at the nondescript house in the southwest quadrant of Portland twenty minutes later. The new woman was black-and-blue around the face, with a nose that had clearly been broken.

"I'm Grey Dawson." Grey extended her hand to the woman. "I'm going to take you to the hospital."

The woman looked at her with large brown eyes full of fear.

"You're safe now," Grey soothed her. "No one can hurt you here."

She guided the woman to her car.

"What's your name?" she asked.

The woman shook her head.

"I understand you're scared, but we're going to have to register you at the emergency room. So you're going to have to tell me your name. Trust me. No one is going to hurt you anymore. Not as long as you stay with us."

"My name is Sally," the woman said through swollen lips.

"Okay, Sally. We're going to get you all taken care of. Just relax and keep that ice on your nose."

They arrived at the hospital, where Grey was greeted by name. She was, unfortunately, a fairly frequent visitor there. They got Sally checked in and sat in the waiting room. Grey held her hand.

"So, do you want to tell me what happened?"

"He got home from the bar and dinner wasn't ready."

"I'm sorry, honey." It was a story Grey had heard before. "This wasn't the first time, was it?"

Sally shook her head.

"You made the right decision, coming to the shelter."

"I had a friend who'd been there. She told me about it."

While Grey appreciated word of mouth, she was sad to think of the conversation the women must have had over and over before Sally got the nerve to walk out of her relationship and into the shelter.

Grey sat with Sally while the doctors set her nose and gave her a prescription for pain pills. They were fortunate that Sally had insurance, which so often wasn't the case with new residents. When they were finished, they filled her prescription and headed back to the shelter.

Grey dropped Sally off and let Cecilia finish the intake process. She headed home, where she poured herself another glass of wine as she got ready for bed.

❖

The party was winding down at Boone's house. She walked the last guests out and was left alone with Dani.

"I'll help you get things cleaned up," Dani said.

They worked comfortably together and put things away and straightened up. Dani moved into Boone's arms.

"You sure know how to throw a party, Fairway."

"Thanks." Boone wrapped her arms around her. "I'm looking forward to the post party, personally."

"As am I." She looked up at Boone, who bent to take her lips in her own.

The kiss was soft and tender. Boone wasn't in any hurry. She knew Dani wasn't going anywhere.

"Let's go back to the hot tub," Boone said.

When they reached the backyard, Boone pulled Dani to her and kissed her again, peeling off her bathing suit as she did. Dani stepped out of her suit and pulled Boone's tank top over her head. Boone slipped off her trunks and took Dani in her arms again. She loved the feel of bare skin against hers. They stepped into the hot tub, the warm water as sensuous as a lover's caress.

Boone pulled Dani onto her lap so she was straddling her. She kissed her again, prying her lips open with her tongue. Her nipples hardened at the feel of Dani's tongue against hers. She felt Dani's intake of breath and kissed her harder, pressing her breasts into Dani's.

Dani wrapped her arms around Boone's shoulders and moved closer. Boone placed her hands on Dani's thighs and gently kneaded them. Her skin was soft and her thighs muscular yet feminine. Boone grew more aroused by the moment. She reached her hands around to cup Dani's ass and slid her closer yet.

She leaned down and took one of Dani's nipples in her mouth. It hardened and Boone ran her tongue over it. She moved to the other nipple and sucked it deep.

Dani took one of Boone's hands and placed it between

her legs. Boone stroked the softness she found there. Dani spread her legs wider and Boone slipped her fingers inside. Dani arched her back and took Boone deeper.

Boone continued to suckle Dani as she moved her fingers in and out. Dani closed her eyes and cried out as Boone took her to her climax.

When Dani stopped shaking, they climbed out of the tub and toweled each other off. Boone led Dani into the bedroom and fell onto her king-size bed with her. Dani climbed on top of Boone and kissed her, her hair fanning out around Boone's face. Boone grabbed her ass and rubbed her all over her stomach. The remnants of Dani's orgasm coated her belly and made her hotter than ever.

Dani scooted lower on her and kissed Boone's breast, taking a nipple in her mouth. She rolled it around on her tongue before moving to the next. She sucked hard on it, and Boone felt the electric currents firing in her clit. She moved on the bed, needing more from Dani, who slid down her body and climbed between her legs.

Boone felt Dani's tongue on her and her head spun. Dani licked her all over, paying close attention to her swollen clit. Boone spread her legs wider and raised her hips, urging more contact.

As Dani continued to work her magic, Boone grew dizzy as the blood rushed to the bundle of nerves at her core. She gripped the sheets and let out a guttural moan as the orgasm coursed through her.

Dani curled up next to Boone, cuddling in her arms. Boone was happy she hadn't had too much to drink. She liked Dani and was comforted knowing she'd know the woman in her bed the next morning.

CHAPTER TWO

"I miss him," Martha Payne said.

Grey sat at her desk, looking at the woman on her couch. She had heard this phrase all too often. She knew she had to be tender yet assertive with the woman. It was a fine line to walk.

"What about him do you miss?" she asked.

"He loves me. And he's really a good person."

Grey stared at the cast on Martha's arm, courtesy of her husband, Bruce.

"Yet look what he did to you."

"I know. But I made him angry."

"Martha, we've talked about this. You really can't take the blame for what happened. And what about if you make him angry again? Who knows what he's capable of? Who knows what he might do next time?"

"I know. And I know I'm free to leave here any time. I know you're right, but I miss him."

"What can we do to help you take your mind off that?"

"I try to keep busy, but clearly I need to do more."

"Have you met with Connie?" Grey knew from her chart that Martha hadn't met with their career planner.

"No."

"I really think you should. A job would give you more confidence in yourself and keep you busy."

"But I've never been to college."

"That's okay. You're a smart, capable woman and you would do well at any job you put your mind to."

"Yeah, if someone would hire me."

"We've got connections in the community, Martha. I'd like to set up a time for you to meet with Connie."

She turned to her computer and scanned the monitor.

"She can see you tomorrow at ten. May I pencil you in?"

"Sure." Martha didn't sound enthusiastic.

"What are your apprehensions? Is it more than your education?"

"I haven't worked in years. What if I don't have skills?"

Grey knew low self-esteem was a constant threat among her residents. They'd been told they were worthless for so long, they started to believe it.

"That's what Connie's for," she said. "She'll evaluate your skills and help match you with a suitable job."

"But we keep hearing there are no jobs in today's economy."

Grey had to fight her frustration. It wasn't an uncommon emotion to feel at her shelter, but she knew she couldn't let it show. "This has to be something you're willing to do, Martha. It'll help build your self-esteem and your independence. Plus, it'll keep you busy and your mind occupied."

"I really have nothing to lose by meeting with her," Martha said.

Well, it was something, anyway. Grey would settle for baby steps. And this was a huge baby step for Martha.

"That's the attitude I want to hear," Grey lied. "You have nothing to lose and so very much to gain."

It was time for their session to end. Grey had more residents to see.

"I'll talk to you Friday and you can let me know how your appointment goes. Sound good?"

"Okay. I'll see you then."

Grey turned back to her computer and jotted down her notes from the session. She closed her eyes and meditated for a few moments, making sure she let go of any negative emotions so she could project positivity to her residents.

Her next session was with Sally, their newest resident. She'd been with them a few days, and Grey had met with her every day. When she walked in, Grey was careful to keep her face neutral and not look shocked at the greens and blues of her face.

"How are you feeling?" Grey asked as she closed the door.

"Embarrassed."

"Embarrassed? How so?"

"I can't believe I let this happen to me."

"You truly believe this was your fault?"

"I do. If I'd had dinner ready, this wouldn't have happened."

"Tell me then, Sally, why didn't you have dinner ready?" Grey asked softly.

Tears that were brimming in Sally's eyes burst loose and flowed freely down her face.

"I'm not agreeing with him, you understand," Grey said. "I'm simply asking what you were doing that prevented you from having dinner ready."

"I was cleaning the house. He insisted we buy a twenty-five-hundred-square-foot house for the two of us, and it takes time to clean it. I'd been doing laundry and cleaning all day. I had dinner going, but it wasn't ready when he got home."

"And he called to let you know he was on his way?"

"No."

"So you had no idea what time you 'had' to have dinner done, did you?"

"No."

"So how can you feel that you were responsible for not getting dinner done in time for him?"

Sally was sobbing. She buried her face in her hands, then jumped at the pain it caused.

"I should have. I just should have."

"And if you'd had it done early and it was cold when he got home, what would have happened?"

Sally looked at her with sad eyes. Grey knew there would have been no way to make her husband happy. She just needed Sally to accept that and release her feelings of responsibility. She changed the subject.

"Have you checked in with your boss?"

Sally nodded and accepted the box of tissues Grey handed her. She wiped her nose and cringed at the pain.

"I told him I'd be out the rest of the week. But I won't be able to take time off after that. How can I go to work looking like this?"

"Did you tell him what happened?"

"No. I told him I'd had an accident and wouldn't be able to go to work."

"Okay, well, we can have someone go in with you this week to talk to him, so he'll at least be aware. How does that sound?"

"That would be good, I guess."

"We'll have a volunteer go with you. When would you like to do that?"

"I'll call my boss to set up an appointment this afternoon."

"Good. Now that that's settled. What would you like to talk about next?"

"What am I going to do?"

"What do you mean?"

"I mean, when I leave here. What am I going to do?"

"Well, there's no hurry, you know that. To leave here, I mean," Grey said.

"But I can't stay here forever."

"You can stay here until you're ready to leave."

"When will that be?" Sally asked.

"Well, each person's stay is different."

"What if someone else needs this place more than me?"

"How can we decide who needs our services more? You need us right now and we're here for you."

"Still, it scares me to think of what lies ahead."

"Why? What specifically scares you?"

"I don't want to go back to him. But where else can I go? You're going to kick me out when my time is up, and I'm not going to have anywhere to go and I'll have to go back. And he's going to be even madder than usual that I've been gone."

Sally was sobbing hysterically. Grey moved to the couch and placed an arm around Sally's shoulder.

"No one's kicking you out," she said. "And no one is going to make you go back to him. We'll start working toward you getting your own place and being able to function on your own."

"But how long will that take?"

"It will take as long as it needs to. There's no time line here, Sally. We're here for you until you're ready. Please don't worry about that. You're welcome to stay here as long as you need to."

Sally leaned against Grey and cried. Grey could feel the tension and fear in her and wished she could do more to reassure her. She simply held her and let her cry.

❖

Boone spent the morning running errands for work. She stopped at the bank to make a deposit, then swung by the butcher's to pick up ground beef for the lunch and dinner rushes. Her week had been slow so far, but they'd had a great weekend, so she didn't worry about the lack of business. And it was Thursday, which meant two-for-one burger night. That always drew a crowd. Plus there was a preseason NFL game on, so she planned on a good night.

She returned to the bar in time for the kitchen crew to make burger patties out of the bulk ground beef she'd bought.

A few people came in around eleven thirty for an early lunch, but the lunch rush hit in earnest at noon. Boone was behind the bar helping pour drinks. They were busy, and she felt good.

"Hey, sis, how about a beer here?"

Boone turned and saw her brother sitting at the bar. He was tall and dark and looked remarkably like her.

"Hey, Tanner! How you doin'?" She handed him his favorite beer. Boone wasn't close to her brother. She wasn't close to anyone in her family, but her brother wasn't an unknown at the bar.

"Are you sticking around? Or is this a one beer kinda stop?"

"Open a tab for me, sis. I'll be here a while."

Boone cringed inside but outwardly kept her cool.

"Sure thing, bro."

She waited on other customers, and when the place cleared out again, she walked back over to Tanner.

"So, how's Phoebe?" She asked about his wife. She was

so quiet and reserved, where Tanner was loud and obnoxious. Boone wondered again how they ever got together.

"She's doing great. Hey, did you see the Ducks on Saturday?"

"You know I did. You have the afternoon off?"

"I'm taking the afternoon off. I work too fucking hard."

Boone bit her tongue. Tanner worked construction, and while she agreed that was hard work, he spent more time at her bar than he should, and she knew The Boonies wasn't the only place he frequented. And he'd borrowed more than a few dollars from her over the years. She doubted he knew what hard work was. She wondered again what that sweet Phoebe saw in him.

"Take a load off, sis. Have a beer with me."

"Maybe just one." She sat down and took a pull on her brew.

"So what's new with you?" he asked.

"Not a thing. Workin' and playin'. That's about it."

"You got a good life, Boone. No responsibilities. No worries. Must be nice."

Boone nearly choked on her beer. No responsibilities? What the hell did he call owning her own business? She really didn't like him sometimes. Well, most of the time. He reminded her a lot of their dad, whom she despised.

"I do have a good life," she said. "But I've worked hard for it. Still do."

"You call this work?" He motioned to the bar. "This is playtime, sis."

"A lot of people do come here to play. And that's a good thing."

"You ready for another beer?" he asked. She found it amusing that he acted like he was buying her beer. She knew there was a ninety percent chance he'd leave without paying his tab. It wouldn't be the first time. Nor the last, unfortunately.

"I've got some things to do," she said. "Be sure to settle up when you're finished."

"You know it."

"I'll catch you later, Tanner."

"Yeah. Later."

She drove back to her house and changed into her swimsuit. She swam laps with determination, trying to relax after seeing her brother. She pushed herself hard so all she could focus on were her strokes as she cut through the water.

Thoughts of Tanner were long gone when she got out of the pool. All she had on her mind was the good time to be had at the bar watching football. She loved fall, and it was rapidly approaching. Summer was still clinging to the Pacific Northwest, a rare treat. But fall would be there soon and that meant even more football. Boone loved all sports, but football was her favorite.

She made it back to the bar at five thirty, in time to watch the pregame show. The place was packed and the kitchen staff were cranking out the two-for-one burgers. Boone smiled. Life was good.

She grabbed a beer and leaned against the bar, leaving the stools open for the paying customers. A group of men came in and asked about the Mariners game. Boone went behind the bar and put the game on a smaller television in the corner. The men were content and sat at a table to watch their team.

The two big screens were dedicated to the football game. The game was between an East Coast team and a Midwest team, so Boone normally wouldn't have cared who won, but the former Ducks coach was leading the Eagles, so she was excited to see how they would fare. Many others in the bar seemed to have the same idea. When Chip Kelly came on the screen, the place erupted in cheers.

The place looked like it did when the Ducks played, with everyone wearing their Ducks gear to support Chip. Now they all had to wait and see if his awesome coaching from college would carry over to the pros.

There were a few people in Kansas City colors, but they were definitely the minority.

Boone made her way around the bar, making sure everyone was having fun and had everything they needed. She wasn't above taking empty pitchers up to the bar to be refilled. Anything to keep the customers happy and coming back.

She wandered over to a table full of Chiefs fans and asked if they were having fun. One young woman smiled at her, her blue eyes twinkling.

"We kind of feel like we're in hostile territory." She laughed.

"Nothing hostile about this place. We're a fun-loving group."

"With a lot of Eagles fans."

"Mostly Duck fans. Rooting for the Eagles 'cause of Chip Kelly."

"Who's he?" the brunette asked.

"Who's Chip Kelly?" Boone laughed. "Only one of the greatest coaches ever in college football."

"I'm sorry. I don't follow college ball."

Boone was at a loss. College ball was huge in Portland. She couldn't imagine anyone not following it.

"You're not from around here, are you?" she asked.

"Did my Chiefs jersey give me away?"

Boone laughed again. She liked this feisty woman with the laughing eyes and beautiful smile. And she liked the way she gave Boone shit. Boone deserved that question and took it in stride.

"I suppose there is that," Boone said. "So how does someone from Kansas City end up watching a game in my lowly bar?"

"*Your* bar?"

"My bar. I own the place." She extended her hand. "I'm Boone."

"Ah. As in The Boonies. Nice to meet you." She took her hand. "I'm Ancella."

"Nice to meet you, Ancella. Let me know if I can get you anything. I'll be making the rounds."

She turned to leave when she felt Ancella's hand on her arm. She looked back.

"Do you have to make the rounds? You're welcome to join us."

"I tell you what. Let me make one more trip around the bar to see that everyone has what they need and then I'll come back and hang out with you."

Boone quickly cruised around the bar, checking for empty glasses and pitchers. She told her waitstaff which tables needed attention, then turned her own attention back to Ancella.

Ancella scooted over on her bench to afford Boone room to sit down. Boone was introduced to the rest of the Chiefs fans at the table and made polite conversation, all the time aware of the nearness of Ancella. She could smell her vanilla musk perfume, and it added to the warmth she was feeling being in her presence.

"So are you from Kansas City?" Boone asked.

"I'm actually from Overland Park, so yeah, pretty much."

"I'll have to take your word on that. I'm not too familiar with Kansas."

"Well, I don't have a dog named Toto or an Auntie Em, if those are your next questions," Ancella said with a smile.

Boone once again laughed at the sharp wit, delivered so effortlessly and in good humor. She liked a smart woman, even if she was a smart-ass.

"Okay, so maybe I know enough about Kansas not to ask that."

"And you?" Ancella said. "Are you Portland born and bred?"

"I actually grew up outside of Eugene and went to college there, then moved here after I graduated."

"Eugene is the home of the Ducks, I take it?"

"Well, you know something about college football, after all."

It was Ancella's turn to laugh.

"No, I just see all these Duck shirts here, so I just assumed you were a Duck, too."

"You're a wise woman, aren't you?"

"I can put two and two together."

Boone stood. "Can I get you all another round?"

She took their orders and walked up to the bar. She ordered their drinks and told the bartender to put it on her tab. Then made sure they knew to get the drinks out to the table immediately.

"You didn't have to do that," Ancella said. "I mean, if you're trying to impress me, relax, I'm already hooked."

"Wow, smart, beautiful, *and* straightforward. I like those qualities in a woman."

"Okay, now you're just being a charmer."

"Can't I be straightforward, too?" Boone said.

"Fair enough," Ancella said. "So, are you one of those fans who has to watch a game until the last play?"

"Are you suggesting we may be able to find something better to do than watch football?"

"I am."

"My truck's out back."

CHAPTER THREE

Oh my God, Boone!" Ancella cried out as she rode Boone's fingers deep inside her. "Oh dear God. I don't know what you're doing, but don't you dare stop!"

"Yeah? You like that? You want more?" Boone plunged her fingers as far as they would go. "You want more of this?"

"Oh God, yes. Please!"

Boone twisted her hand and stroked a different area in the depths of Ancella. The soft, silky area was very responsive, no matter where she rubbed her fingertips. Her pussy was tight, squeezing Boone, but Boone reveled in the feeling. She knew her knuckles rubbing against Ancella pleased her as much as her fingers.

Ancella arched her hips, taking her deeper. She thrust them round and round, allowing Boone to touch every spot inside her.

"Holy fuck, Boone. You sure know what you're doing."

Encouraged, Boone continued to fuck her with all she had.

"You're so fucking hot," Boone said. "Oh God, you're fun."

"I can't take much more," Ancella said.

"I bet you can."

"No, please. I need to come, Boone. Please get me off."

Boone focused her attention on the soft plushness at her fingertips and flicked her fingers against it. Her hand was cramping, yet she still gave it her all.

"Come for me, Ancella. Come for me now."

"Oh yes, Boone. Oh dear God, YES!" she screamed.

Boone braced herself as Ancella's center closed around her over and over, bruising her in its intensity. It was a small price to pay to give her such pleasure.

"How you doing?" Boone asked a few minutes later.

Ancella nodded.

"I'm going to pull my hand out now."

Ancella nodded again.

Boone slowly withdrew her hand, happy at last to have it free of its confines. She lay next to Ancella and wrapped her arms around her.

"I don't think I have any liquid left in my body," Ancella said with a thick tongue. Boone laughed and handed her a glass of water.

"Much better. Thank you," Ancella said.

"I aim to please."

"You succeed."

"Thank you."

Boone pulled Ancella into her arms again and they fell into a fitful sleep.

Ancella shook Boone awake in the morning.

"Hey, handsome? Boone?"

"Hmm?" Sleep had a solid grip on Boone.

"Hey, Boone. I hate to do this, but I need to get home to get ready for work. I left my car at the bar. I need a ride. Boone? Are you awake?"

Boone stretched, the night before coming back to her.

"You sure you need to go right now?"

"I'm sorry, but I really do."

Boone finally opened her eyes and saw that Ancella was already dressed.

"So I guess a repeat performance is out of the question, huh?"

"Sorry, lover boi. I need to get going."

Boone got up and got dressed quickly.

"And in the future?" she asked.

"What? Oh a repeat performance? I'd be a fool to turn down another night like last night."

"Well, don't be a stranger at the bar," Boone said.

"I won't. But don't worry. Just because I show up won't mean I'm stalking you."

Boone laughed again. She really enjoyed Ancella.

"Fair enough. Okay, let's get you to your car."

❖

After she dropped Ancella at her car, Boone headed home for more shuteye before work. She woke later, showered, and made it back to the bar by eleven to help with the lunch rush.

"Hey, lover girl. How was your night?" Christopher asked.

"It was good. How was yours?"

"Well, I came down here to watch the game and you weren't around."

"No. I left pretty early."

"So I heard."

"Some things are more important than football, my man."

"Some hot women are, for sure!"

"So, are we all ready for the rush?" Boone asked.

"We are. It's Friday, so that means a lot of our lunch rush will stick around through happy hour."

"I love Fridays."

"Speaking of Fridays, you got something interesting in the mail today," Christopher said. He walked over to the pile of mail behind the bar and handed her a postcard.

"What's this?" she said, then read it. "Oh, no. No way. I'm not going."

"When was the last time you went to a Chamber of Commerce mixer?" Christopher asked.

"Not long enough ago. Those things are so boring."

"Free food, free drink, and a chance to promote the bar. It's a no-brainer. You have to go."

"Remind me again who the boss is here?"

"Come on, Boone. It's good to be seen by the movers and shakers."

Deep down, Boone knew he was right. She'd go, have a few cocktails, shake a few hands, then make a quick exit. Fortunately, she had a week to mentally prepare for it.

❖

"Sally left this morning," Cecilia told Grey when she got to work Friday morning.

"Shit. Where'd she go?"

"Home."

The word hit Grey like a blow to the gut. It wasn't the first time this had happened, and it certainly wouldn't be the last. Yet each time it happened, it knocked the wind out of her. She sat at her desk and buried her face in her hands.

"She didn't even give us a fair shot," Grey said. "We really could have helped her."

"She sure needed us," Cecilia said.

Grey leaned back, absorbing the news.

She didn't say what they were both thinking. Sally would be back. Only how bad a shape would she be in the next time they saw her?

"Any other great news you have for me today?"

"Martha met with Connie yesterday. You have an appointment with her today to see how it went."

"Have you talked to Connie?"

"Yes. Martha is still resistant."

"I'll have a good session with her," Grey said.

"She's first on your agenda."

"Well, then I'd better get to it."

She walked down the hall to the room she used for visits with residents. Martha walked in soon after.

"How did your meeting with Connie go?"

"I don't know," Martha said.

"You don't know?"

"I guess it went well. I'm just still not convinced."

"What did you and Connie talk about?"

"She asked me what I wanted to do. What sort of career I might want."

"And what did you say?"

"I laughed. Then cried. I'll never have a career."

"Martha, tell me one of your strengths."

"I don't have any. I used to think I was a good wife, but we all know better now."

"We need to get you to stop blaming yourself for what happened. How could that have been your fault?" Grey knew deep down Martha had to know that or she would have stayed with her husband. The thing was getting her to realize she knew that.

"Name another strength."

"I don't have any."

"Let's try this. What did you want to be when you were a little girl? What was your dream?"

Martha started sobbing.

"What is it?"

"I just wanted to be a wife and mommy. Now I'll never be a mommy."

"You don't know that," Grey said.

"I'm used goods."

"You're an attractive young woman who will someday be ready to start again."

"I'm not attractive, and I'm not so young anymore."

"How old are you?" Grey asked.

"Twenty-seven."

"You really think that's too old to start over?"

"I thought we were talking about me getting a job."

"This is. We need to know about your hopes and dreams to help you find a job that will work for you."

"I don't have any hopes or dreams. Why can't you people understand that?"

"Okay then, let's talk about your likes and dislikes. I know you've been helping a lot in the kitchen here and helping with childcare. You could pursue either of those fields."

"And what do I put on my application?" Martha asked. "Worked with children at the shelter for abused women?"

"Being here is nothing to be ashamed of. It means you're smart and strong enough to step out of a dangerous situation so you can improve your life. You're doing the right thing, Martha. And we can help get you started in either of those fields."

Martha stopped crying. She wiped her eyes with the tissues Grey handed her.

"Maybe that is something I could do."

"Excellent. That's what I like to hear. Promise me you'll talk to Connie about that at your appointment on Monday."

"I promise."

"Good. Thank you. Okay, Martha, our time is up for today. My door is always open if you need me, though. Please keep that in mind."

Martha nodded and stood to leave. "Thank you, Grey. You and everybody for all you're doing for me."

"You're more than welcome."

Martha left and Grey did her usual meditation. Then she went in search of Cecilia.

"Anything I need to know about?" Grey asked.

Cecilia handed her a postcard.

"What's this?" Grey read it. "Oh, fantastic. The Chamber of Commerce mixer. That's great. It'll be good to spread the word about Serene Pathway. We'll get more companies interested and maybe find more sponsors and get more donations."

"I knew you'd be happy to see that."

"I am. Oh, this makes my day." She entered the event on her phone.

The office phone rang and Cecelia answered it. "Serene Pathway. How may I help you?"

Grey saw her stiffen.

"No, of course. We can help you." She sat quietly. "Of course your children are welcome."

Grey leaned back in her chair. It never ended.

"How many children do you have? Yes, we have room. Where are you now?" She scribbled an address down. "I can be there in ten minutes. Just stay put and you can follow me here."

"What's going on?" Grey asked when Cecilia hung up.

"I have to go get her. Mom with two kids."

"What happened?"

"She didn't want to talk in front of the kids."

"Okay. I'll go let Tonya know she may have two new kids to counsel. I'll talk to the woman as soon as you guys get back."

"I'll be back."

Grey wandered down the hall to Tonya's office. Tonya was a licensed child therapist. Fortunately, her services in that capacity weren't needed too often.

"Knock, knock," Grey said.

Tonya looked up from her paperwork.

"Come on in. What's going on?"

"We've got a new woman coming in. Cecilia went to pick her up. She's got two kids with her. She wouldn't say anything over the phone in front of them. So we don't know what they've seen. It may have been pretty gruesome. Or it may be nothing. We'll let you know when we know something."

"I'll check my schedule and rearrange it to see them if you deem that necessary."

"Thanks. I appreciate it."

Cecilia arrived moments later with a petite woman with long dark hair and scared brown eyes.

"I'm Grey." She held out her hand.

"This is Virginia," Cecilia said.

Grey eyed the two small children hiding in the woman's skirt. She bent to their level and smiled. "And who might you be?"

The children retreated behind their mother. Grey wondered anew what horror these kids had witnessed. She stood upright again and looked Virginia in the eye.

"I'd like to hear your story as soon as I can. Are the little ones scared or shy?"

"A little of both."

"Would they like to play with some other children, do you think?"

"Maybe. But I don't know that they'll want to be away from me right now."

"And that's okay," Grey said. "We'll talk when they're ready. We do have a play room if they'd like to go see it?"

"Let's go take a look at the play room, kiddos." Virginia placed her hands behind their heads and urged them in front of her so she could take their hands.

Grey turned to Cecilia. "Why don't you go see if Tonya can meet us there?"

Grey led the way down the hall. There were only a few children playing in the room, and the television was on in the background. "Do either of you like movies? We can put a movie in for you."

"Would you like that?" Virginia asked.

Tonya walked in then and introduced herself to Virginia.

"Why don't we all sit here on this couch for a few minutes?" Tonya said. "You heard me tell your mommy my name. Now will you tell me yours?"

The children looked up at Virginia with wide eyes.

"It's okay. Tonya is our new friend. You can tell her your names."

"My name's Jock," the little boy said.

"I'm Emma."

"Well, it's very nice to meet both of you. I'd like to stay here with you while your mommy goes and talks to Grey for a while. How would you feel about that?"

"Will Mommy be okay?" Jock asked.

"Of course. Why wouldn't she be?" Tonya asked.

Jock looked up at Tonya and a tear rolled down his cheek. "We keep her safe."

"Well, Grey will keep her safe, too. I promise."

Grey escorted Virginia down the hall.

"Please, have a seat." She pointed to the sofa.

Virginia sat down, wringing her hands.

"So, you want to give me some history or just tell me what happened to bring you here?"

"First of all, is there a rule about how long I stay? We'll really only need to be here until I can get a place of my own. I'm not hurting financially."

"That's fine. Stay as long or short as you like. Bear in mind we do offer counseling services for you and the kids while you're here."

"I appreciate that."

"Okay, so what brings you here?"

"He's always been mean. He pushes me, shoves me, swears at me. I've known for a while that I needed to get away."

"What was the final straw?"

"He pulled the butcher's knife on me last night. I was terrified. I don't know what would have happened if Jock hadn't come in. My husband told me he didn't want his son to see him hurt me. So he put the knife down. I slept with the kids last night then left the house and called you as soon as he left for work this morning."

"I'm glad you called. So have the children witnessed the pushing and shoving?"

Virginia nodded.

"It's okay. Tonya is a licensed child therapist. She can talk to them."

"I really don't think I'll be here that long. I'll get them set up with private counseling. I don't want to sound unappreciative. I just want to be honest with you."

"That's fine. Just know the services are here if you need them."

"Thank you. Thank you so much for what you do."

"You're quite welcome. Now let's get you to your room."

CHAPTER FOUR

Thursday night was jumping at The Boonies. Boone was excited to see everyone enjoying their dinners and loved having football on the big screen. This week Seattle was playing, and the place was packed. She made her usual rounds of the bar, picking up empty pitchers and glasses and scouting for any potential bedmates for the night.

Football night was a predominantly male event, but having the closest thing to a home team playing that night meant a lot of women as well as men filling the tables. She spotted an attractive woman with long blond hair sitting with a large group. She changed her course to approach the table when Dani stepped in front of her.

"Hey, stud."

"Hey, Dani."

"Busy night," Dani said.

"Yeah, it's a great crowd." Boone looked past Dani and saw the blonde looking her way.

"Well, I'll let you get back to work. I just wanted to say hi."

Boone favored her with a wide smile. "Well, thanks. It's great to see you."

When Dani walked off, Boone continued her route to the

blonde, who stood as she approached. Boone smiled and was just about to say something when the blonde stepped around her and threw her arms around a tall, hulking young man. She planted a big kiss on him, and Boone felt her libido deflate. But it didn't cool her spirits. Life was good. She could just cross the blonde off her list for the night.

Boone sat with a table of regulars to watch the game. By halftime, Boone was feeling no pain. She had a nice buzz going, plus the game was tight, so no one was leaving early. It was a good night.

The gang at Boone's table was rowdy, and she joined them in yelling at the television, rooting for the Seahawks. She'd left the bussing of tables and taking orders to the waitstaff to just relax and enjoy the camaraderie.

Late in the fourth quarter, Dani came over and sat next to her.

"Great game, huh?"

"Too close for comfort," Boone said.

"I hope I'm not sitting too close for comfort," Dani joked.

Boone put her arm around her. "No such thing where you're concerned, darlin'."

They stayed that way for most of the rest of the game, although they separated and stood to cheer when the Seahawks kicked a last second field goal to win the game.

Then Boone pulled Dani into a big hug and kissed her cheek.

"How 'bout those Seahawks?" Boone said.

"Yeah! How 'bout them?"

"You ready to get out of here?" Boone asked.

"Sure am."

They drove to Boone's house and started undressing each other as soon as the door closed behind them. In between kisses, they stripped one another of their shirts, shorts, bras, and underwear.

"God, your body's hot," Dani said. "You're so tall and lean and I just want you."

"I want you, too. And I plan to have you. Every way I can."

They made their way to the bedroom and fell into bed. Boone wrapped her arms around Dani, her mouth kissed her passionately. Boone moved her hand to Dani's center and buried her fingers.

"You're so fucking hot," Boone moaned. She moved in and out while she moved her mouth to Dani's hard nipple. She sucked deeply and licked the hard nub. She lost herself in the feeling of Dani's body around her.

Dani reached her hand between her own legs and grabbed Boone's wrist, pumping it inside her. Boone felt her own pussy clench at the feeling. Dani was so uninhibited, which made her such a fun playmate.

Boone sucked harder at Dani's nipple and heard her scream her name as she came.

"You need to touch me, baby," Boone whined. "I need you so fucking bad."

Dani deftly rubbed Boone's swollen clit as Boone arched her back and moved her hips. She felt the orgasm approaching and closed her eyes to focus all her attention.

"Oh God!" she cried. "Oh Jesus Christ, yes!"

❖

Friday morning, Boone walked into the bar with a spring in her step.

"Someone's in a good mood today," Christopher said.

"It's a beautiful day." Boone poured herself some coffee then pulled her laptop out of the safe.

"I thought maybe you were just excited about the mixer tonight."

"The what? Oh shit. That's tonight?"

"Yes, it is. And you're going."

"I'd better start drinking now," Boone said.

"You'd better be sober when you get there," Christopher said.

"What's your deal with this mixer thing?" Boone asked.

"I just think it's a great way to expand our clientele."

"What's wrong with the clientele we have now? This place was packed last night."

"What about a regular Tuesday night? Right after work. It would be nice to see more business people stopping by for happy hour before they head home."

"We have people stopping by is all I'm saying."

"We could have more is all I'm saying."

Boone looked up from her laptop. "Are you saying you want to turn this into a hipster bar or something?"

"Businessmen and women aren't hipsters."

"I know, but yuppie sounds so dated," Boone said.

"It is."

"And we have a lot of young business people that come in here."

"Why are you so against making more money?" Christopher asked.

"I'm not. I'm just not sure a Chamber of Commerce mixer is the way to do it."

"And I'm saying it's free, it's easy, so why not?"

"Fine. I said I'd go and I will, but know I'm doing it under protest."

"Duly noted."

"Hey, I've got an idea," Boone said. "Why don't you go and represent The Boonies?"

"Because these aren't for the hired help. They're for the owners. And that, like it or not, is you."

❖

Grey stepped out of the shower after a long day at work and dressed in a red skirt and a short-sleeved white blouse. She checked herself out in the mirror and was pleased that she looked professional yet casual. She looked approachable, yet nice enough to represent Serene Pathway and all that meant. She slipped on some red pumps, grabbed her purse, and headed out the door.

She arrived at the convention center and found her name tag on the table. She proudly taped it to her blouse and walked in the room. She felt good, her confidence in place. She just needed to start mingling.

Most people were congregated around the drink table, so she walked over and helped herself to a glass of white wine. A tall balding man who looked to be in his early forties was the first to speak to her.

"Mike Thomas from Valley Bank." He offered his hand.

"Grey Dawson from Serene Pathway."

"So I see. What is that?"

"We're a shelter for abused women."

"Is that right? How come I've never heard of you?"

"We're more a word of mouth kind of place. For the protection of our residents, we don't publicize our place."

"And yet you're here," Mike said.

"I'm looking for sponsors and donations. We always need those."

"What kind of advertising do your sponsors get?"

"Unfortunately, we can't offer anything like that."

"That's too bad. You sound like a good cause."

"We count on people wanting to help the good cause," Grey said.

"Do you have a card or something? I can always ask the bean counters if we could sponsor you."

Grey handed Mike a business card.

"I hope you can convince them. We can always use more financial support."

"I'm sure you can."

Mike walked off and Grey turned toward the door. Her breath caught. In walked the most handsome woman Grey had seen in a very long time. Tall and trim, with short dark hair, she carried herself with ease and comfort. Grey was intrigued.

❖

Boone entered the room, full of dread and already counting down until she'd be able to leave. She'd promised Christopher to press some flesh and she would. But not much. These didn't look like her type of people. But she understood Christopher's point. New people meant potential new customers, which meant more money. She took a deep breath and started toward the drink table.

As she neared the table, she felt herself being watched. It was then she noticed the woman with the shoulder length auburn hair and dark green eyes. Boone's mood improved. She asked for a beer and turned to the woman, who was by then involved in a conversation with another woman. Patience, Boone told herself. She'd get there.

A man walked up to Boone.

"Hi, I'm Jeff Holiday, Holiday Hardware."

"Nice to meet you. Boone Fairway, The Boonies."

"What's that?"

"It's a sports bar over on Hawthorne."

"Nice. Any specials you have?"

"Happy hour every day from three to seven and two-for-one burgers every Thursday night."

"Right on. I'm always looking for a new place to check out."

"Well, please check us out. And bring some friends." She smiled.

"I will. Nice to meet you, Boone."

"Nice meeting you, too."

As he moved past her Boone saw the attractive woman standing by herself. She quickly closed the distance between them. She saw the woman's eyes brighten and watched a flush cover her cheeks, both good signs.

"Hello…" She read her name tag. "Grey. What an unusual name."

"Thank you. I see you have an interesting name, as well."

"I do. So, let's make it official." She offered her hand. "Boone Fairway."

"Grey Dawson." She shook her hand.

"And, Grey, you're with Serene Pathway. I'm not familiar."

"We're a shelter for abused women."

"What a fantastic cause. Although that must be such hard work."

"It's very hard work. But so rewarding."

"What exactly do you do there?"

"Well, I run the place, so I do whatever's necessary. But I also counsel the residents."

"My hat's off to you. I'm honored to have met you."

"And, Boone, you own The Boonies," Grey said. "What's that?"

Boone puffed out her chest with pride.

"It's a sports bar over on Hawthorne."

"A sports bar?" Grey's demeanor changed.

"Sure. Why?"

"Do you have any idea how many of my residents end up there as a result of their husbands or partners coming home from a sports bar?"

"Hey, now," Boone said. "That's not fair."

"What's not?"

"To color me as the bad guy for what a few people have done."

"A *few* people? Domestic violence is an epidemic. One in four women will have experienced some form of domestic abuse in their lifetime. That's not a few, Ms. Fairway."

"And you're telling me that hanging out at a sports bar is going to make a person abusive?"

"I'm telling you I've heard of that happening more than once. Now, if you'll excuse me."

"Wait. I really don't think you're giving me a fair shake," Boone said.

Grey reached into her purse and pulled out a business card.

"If you ever want to see what your innocent patrons are doing to women, give me a call."

Boone stood fuming as she watched her leave. She tucked the card in her pocket, knowing she'd never look at it again.

Her mood spoiled, she was determined to put on a smile and work the crowd some more, but it wasn't easy. Not only had those beautiful eyes and warm smile turned hard and cold against her, Grey had brought up memories Boone fought hard to keep buried deep.

She found herself wondering where shelters like Serene Pathway were when she was growing up. Her mom could have used their services, to be sure. Maybe they'd been around, but no one told her mom where they were.

She shook the thoughts from her mind and grabbed another beer. She mingled and talked up her bar for another hour before giving up and heading home.

❖

Grey sat in her car trying to compose herself. She couldn't believe she let herself get so riled up at that Fairway woman. Grey knew there was a lot of ambiguity in the connection between alcohol and abuse. Alcohol didn't necessarily cause the abuse; men just used it to justify their behavior. Still, she'd seen too many cases of women abused at the hands of a man who just got home from a bar not to come to her own conclusions.

And that Boone woman seemed to think she was innocent in the whole scheme of things. Like her patrons would never do anything like that. Grey wondered how many of Boone's patrons went home at night and beat up their wives. But as long as Boone didn't see it, she probably didn't care.

Well, let her stay all smug and handsome and happy. Grey vowed not to give her a second thought, but the whole drive home, she thought of those haunting blue eyes and dimpled smile. It almost made her sad to think she'd never see them again.

CHAPTER FIVE

Boone got to the bar early Saturday morning, since the Ducks game started at ten, when the bar opened. She made sure everything was ready and greeted the partiers as they poured in as soon as she opened the doors. She was in a good mood, though thoughts of Grey and her words still haunted her. She tried not to think about her patrons abusing their partners and spouses, but couldn't help but wonder now. She cautioned her bartenders against overserving, just in case.

She settled at a table with some regulars and watched her Ducks again rout their opponents. She was proud of her team and was in a fantastic space by the end of the game. She invited the regulars to come over to her place for a swim and barbecue. She knew the nice weather wouldn't be around much longer, and she wanted to take advantage of it by keeping the party going.

Boone was working at the grill when she noticed a woman she didn't recognize climb out of her pool. The woman had long blond hair that curled around her ample breasts. Boone was mesmerized by the drops of water rolling down her breasts. Or maybe she was just mesmerized by the breasts. Either way, she knew she had to meet the beauty.

She crossed to the pool and squatted next to the woman, who was now perched on the edge of the pool.

"I don't think we've met. I'm Boone."

"Oh, this is your place, huh? I'm Sasha. I'm friends with Dante. He said you wouldn't mind if I came over, too."

"I don't mind at all. You're more than welcome here." She flashed her best smile.

Sasha smiled back.

"I'd better get back to my grilling," Boone said. "I'll talk to you later?"

"Count on it."

Boone walked back to her grill and flipped the dogs and burgers.

"She's hot," Dani said.

"Hey, Dani. I didn't know you were here."

"I never miss a Boone Fairway pool party."

"True."

"So, do you think she'd like to join us?"

"Join us?"

"Sure. I was thinking the three of us might have some fun later on," Dani said.

"Hey, Dani, I like you a lot and all, but every time we see each other, it doesn't mean we're going to end up in bed."

"Oh, I know. And if you want her to yourself, that's cool. I just thought it would be fun. Think about it."

Boone did think about it and thought that having two lovely ladies in her bed did sound like fun.

"I'm just not sure she'd go for it. I mean, it sounds good to me, but I don't want to blow a chance with her."

"Let me feel her out," Dani said.

"As long as I get to feel her up." Boone laughed.

Dani walked off as Boone pulled the meat off the grill. She placed everything on a platter and let everyone serve up at their leisure. She walked back over to Sasha, who was now lying on a lounge, sunning herself.

"The food's ready," Boone said. "Would you like me to fix you a plate?"

"I'll get it when I'm ready. Why don't we just visit for a while?"

"Sure thing. So what do you do, Sasha?"

"I'm a financial analyst."

"Wow. Sounds important," Boone said.

"It's actually exciting. I get to play games with other people's money. It's fun."

Boone had to laugh at the mention of games. Although the games she was planning on playing with Sasha had nothing to do with money.

"Well, I guess that's one way to look at it. Still, sounds like a lot of pressure."

"Sure, but there are lots of ways to relieve pressure, too, you know."

"I'm aware. And I'm a fan of many ways to relieve pressure."

"What's your favorite?" Sasha asked.

Boone felt the blush before she said a word.

"I really feel like I should get to know you better before I tell you that," she said.

"Oh, I think I know you well enough to hear it."

"I need to go check on other guests now." Boone stood. "It was nice chatting with you."

"I'm sure we'll chat again soon," Sasha said.

Boone circulated through the group, stopping to chat with her regulars and meet some guests they'd brought. The mood was festive and people had started to help themselves to the food. She loved her life.

Dani was by her side again.

"Things look promising for you," she said.

"So far, so good," Boone said.

"She's been watching you, you know."

"I didn't know, but thank you." She was all smiles.

Dani left her to mingle, and Boone turned and literally bumped into Sasha. The feel of that warm, soft flesh pressing into her made her crotch clench.

"I'm sorry," Boone said.

"Don't be." Sasha smiled. "So is she your date?"

"What? Who?"

"That redhead. I've seen her watching you all afternoon."

So Sasha really had been watching her. She smiled at the thought.

"So is she your date or not?"

"Not exactly."

"But she has been."

"Sure. But there's nothing between us. I mean, nothing serious, you know."

"Okay. I just wondered if you were taken."

"No, I'm not. At all."

"Well, I'm thinking she wants you tonight," Sasha said.

Boone thought long and hard about how to answer. This was the opening she'd been hoping for.

"She might."

"She's cute."

"She is. Why are you asking? Are you interested?"

"In her or you?" Sasha asked.

"Either. Or both."

"Both?" Sasha raised her eyebrows. "Now that's an interesting proposition."

"Is it?" Boone's heart raced. She realized she was holding her breath and warned herself to play it cool.

"It really is." Sasha walked off in the direction of Dani, leaving Boone to wonder what her night might turn into.

She turned back to the food but found she was too excited to eat. She grabbed another beer, hoping to calm her nerves. She drank it fast and grabbed another one. She scanned the crowd hoping she wasn't obvious, looking for either of her prospects for later that evening. She saw neither and wondered if that was a good sign or not.

One of the guys, a regular from the bar, walked up behind her and pushed Boone into the pool. He jumped in after her, calling, "Water fight!"

Several others jumped in, and soon Boone found herself engaged in a battle of splashing between close to twenty people. She splashed and was splashed for the next ten minutes, when people finally got tired of water in their faces.

She laughed as she climbed out of the pool and gladly accepted the towel that was handed to her. Everyone else got out of the pool as well, and soon people were lounging around again, drinking beer and drying off.

"You should get out of those wet clothes," Sasha whispered in her ear.

Boone felt her nipples tighten under her wet T-shirt and hoped they weren't too obvious.

"I'll dry off out here in the sun."

"So when does the post party start?" Sasha asked.

"When everyone else is gone."

"And whoever's left gets to play?"

"I guess that depends on who's left."

"I certainly hope I'm invited."

"I'd love to engage in a little post-party play time with you."

"Good. Because I'm planning on that."

The guests left and Boone started cleaning up, with Dani and Sasha helping her. She was shaking in anticipation of what was to come, but tried to focus on the task at hand. She was washing a plate when Sasha walked up behind her, wrapping her arms around her middle. Boone couldn't focus. All she knew was the feel of Sasha's breasts pressed against her back.

Sasha kissed the back of Boone's neck, and Boone felt her legs go weak. Her stomach fluttered. She needed this woman intensely.

Boone turned and took Sasha in her arms. Dani was forgotten as she kissed Sasha's soft lips, prying them open with her tongue. She was dizzy with need as their tongues met. She placed her hand on the back of Sasha's head and held her in place as their kiss heated up.

Boone felt a hand on her breast at the same time she felt Dani licking her earlobe. The sensations were almost overwhelming. Dani spun her around and kissed her, leaving Sasha to run her hands under Boone's shirt and along her taut belly. Boone felt her stomach muscles twitch at the touch.

Boone found her mouth alone when Dani moved her out of the way to kiss Sasha. Watching the women kiss did little to ease the fire burning deep inside her. She wanted them both and wanted them at that moment.

"Let's go to my room," Boone said.

"We're still getting warmed up," Sasha said.

"I don't know how much warmer I could get," Boone said.

Dani laughed. "Easy, Turbo. We'll get there."

Boone didn't like being put off, but she had to admit, she could watch them make out for a little longer. And make out they did. Dani kissed Sasha again, this time removing her bathing suit top as she did.

Not wanting to be left out, Boone turned Sasha away from Dani and placed her hand over a large bare breast. The skin was soft and filled her hand perfectly. She bent and licked the nipple, watching it grow. Dani bent to take the other nipple in her mouth and Sasha mewled, letting them know how they were making her feel.

Boone let Dani continue to suckle Sasha. She stood and unhooked the back of Dani's bikini top. When her breasts fell free, Boone reached out and coddled them. She twirled the nipples between her thumbs and forefingers. She tugged and twisted them and felt Dani sag against her in her excitement.

Sasha pulled Dani to a standing position and pressed their breasts together so they were nipple to nipple.

"Oh shit, that's hot," Boone breathed.

Dani moved side to side to rub her nipples against Sasha's. Boone watched in amazement at the sheer sexiness of it.

"It feels so good," Dani said before kissing Sasha again.

They broke the kiss and Sasha pulled Boone to her, kissing her and running her hand down the back of Boone's swim trunks. Boone shivered at the feel of Sasha's hand on her flesh.

"You're so toned," Sasha whispered against her mouth.

Boone felt her trunks being lowered and felt Dani reach around to massage her slick clit. Her knees buckled and she fought to remain upright.

She struggled to get Sasha's bottoms off her and reached between her legs to stroke her.

"Holy shit, you're wet," Boone said.

"Let me feel," Dani said, pressing against Boone's back as she moved her hand to Sasha.

Boone reached behind her to feel Dani's wetness, but found her suit bottom still on.

"You need to get out of this," Boone said.

"Good idea." Dani stepped out of her bikini bottom and grabbed Boone's hand, spinning her around as she placed it on her center.

Boone slipped her fingers inside Dani as she kissed her hard on her mouth. She felt Sasha's hand on her. She wanted more of them than she was able to get in the kitchen.

"Come on." Boone took their hands. "Let's go to the bedroom."

They fell onto the bed, Sasha pulling Boone to her for a kiss. Boone was almost lost in the moment until she felt Dani's tongue on her clit.

"Ohh." She groaned into Sasha's mouth. She rolled onto her back, opening her legs. She pulled Sasha to her, taking a nipple in her mouth. Boone sucked hard on it, feeling it poking the roof of her mouth. She held the breast in both hands, kneading as she suckled greedily.

She kissed down Sasha's belly, ever aware of Dani working her magic between her legs. She was teetering and fought to hold on as she maneuvered Sasha so she could put her tongue inside her. Sasha tasted delicious, salty and sweet, and Boone licked every inch of her.

Boone was so close to her own orgasm, but was determined to make Sasha come first. It wasn't going to happen, she soon realized as the lights burst behind her eyelids and her body convulsed in the fit of her climax.

She continued to lick Sasha as she felt Dani move up next to them. Dani placed Boone's hand on her clit and Boone rubbed it. She did her best to focus on both women, and finally Sasha cried out as she came.

Sasha switched her position to suck on Dani's nipple and Boone moved her mouth to Dani, who took very little time before she screamed as the orgasm rolled over her.

They collapsed together into a fitful sleep.

CHAPTER SIX

The beginning of the next week was uneventful until Wednesday. Boone arrived at work that morning and started preparing her deposit for the day when there was a pounding on the front door. She ignored it, thinking it was an overzealous patron. It was only nine o'clock, so whoever it was would have to wait another hour.

She continued to work, but the pounding went on. She stood to walk to the door to tell the person to leave when her cell rang.

"Hello?" she said.

The voice on the other end was garbled.

"I'm sorry. I can't understand you," Boone said.

The person seemed to be crying and mumbling. Boone struggled, but still couldn't understand them. She was about to hang up when the person yelled through the phone.

"Phoebe!"

"Phoebe? Is this you? I can't understand you, honey," she told her sister-in-law.

"Door!" the person yelled.

Boone moved quickly and opened her front door to find Phoebe standing there with her face colored a sick purplish hue and her lips busted open. She pulled her to her in a hug.

She pulled Phoebe inside and wet a towel to press to her lips.

"Oh my God, Phoebe. What happened to you?"

"Tanner."

Boone had a sick feeling in her gut. She should have expected this from her brother. He was a grade A asshole, but she'd hoped he was different from their father in at least one aspect. Now she knew better.

"I'm so sorry," she said.

Phoebe was still sobbing and holding the towel to her lips. She took a deep breath and moved the towel.

"I'm sorry. I didn't know where else to go."

"It's okay. You did the right thing coming to me." Grey's face flashed in her head. "I know someone who can help and a safe place for you. Are you interested?"

Phoebe's eyes were wide, and Boone could see her fear.

"It's a place Tanner will never find you," Boone said. "I'd let you stay with me, but eventually, he'd come looking for you. You don't want him to find you, do you?"

Phoebe shook her head.

"Okay. So we need to swing by my place really fast and then we'll get you to a doctor."

Phoebe nodded and allowed Boone to steer her out of the building and into her truck. She helped her inside her house, and Boone ran to her bedroom, frantically trying to recall what she'd worn to the mixer the previous week. She remembered and dug through her pockets to find Grey's card.

She hurried back to Phoebe and they drove to a Convenient Care walk-in clinic. While they waited to be seen, Boone called Serene Pathway.

"May I speak to Grey, please?" she asked the person who answered the phone. "Yes, this is Boone Fairway."

"Boone, to what do I owe this pleasure?" Grey's voice was cold on the other end of the line.

"Grey, I need your help. I'm with my sister-in-law. My brother did quite a number on her." She softened her voice. "Please help us."

"Where are you?"

"At the Convenient Care in Southwest."

"I'll get there as soon as I can. What's your sister-in-law's name?"

"Phoebe."

"I'll ask for her if you're in a room already."

"Thank you, Grey."

❖

Grey grabbed an intake packet from the file cabinet and hurried out the door. She was concerned about what state Phoebe must be in for Boone to have called her. And despite the circumstances, a small part of her was also excited about getting to see Boone again. She knew it was inappropriate to be feeling that way, but she couldn't help it. Boone had sounded so sad and worried on the phone. Grey just wanted to wrap her arms around her and tell her it was going to be okay. She hoped it would be.

She arrived at the Convenient Care and found them still in the waiting room. Boone stood.

Grey took in the sight of Boone. Gone was the cocky, confident bar owner. She was clearly shaken. She held the hand of the badly beaten woman hunched over in the chair. When their eyes met, she saw real fear in Boone.

Grey fought her desire to comfort Boone. If it weren't for establishments like The Boonies, she'd see less of this kind of treatment of women. She shook off her train of thought. It wasn't only bars that caused this, and resentment wasn't what these women needed. After all, Boone had reached out to her, and she needed to put aside her disapproval of her business. She needed to focus and be present for Phoebe and Boone.

"Thank you so much for coming. Phoebe, this is Grey. She runs a shelter for abused women."

Phoebe stared at her blankly, fear still apparent in her eyes. Grey placed a hand on her shoulder.

"It's going to be okay, Phoebe. We'll get you taken care of. I need to ask you a few questions. Do you think you'll be able to answer them?"

Phoebe looked at Boone, who looked back to Grey.

"Her lips are pretty bad. Talking isn't that easy for her right now."

Grey nodded. She'd experienced this before. Too many times.

"How about if I ask you questions and you can nod or shake your head?"

Phoebe moved the towel from her mouth and Grey fought not to show her reaction to the torn, bloodied lips.

"I'll try to talk," Phoebe said.

"I'll step away so you two can talk in private," Boone said.

Phoebe grabbed her hand. "No! Please, stay."

"I don't know." Boone hesitated. "This could get pretty personal."

"Please?" Phoebe looked terrified.

"Fine. I'll stay. But promise me you'll let me know when you want me to leave."

Phoebe nodded.

Grey went through the packet, asking Phoebe for details about the incident that brought her there, as well as explaining the services her shelter provided. She tried to focus on Phoebe as she described the attack, but sensed Boone tensing up. She looked up, and the look of anger on Boone's face was hard to ignore. Her chiseled face was tight and her lips drawn in a thin line. Grey wished she could do something to help her, but she was there for Phoebe. She knew from experience the anger would do nothing to help right now, and in fact could be detrimental to Phoebe's recovery. If she realized she was creating such a reaction in Boone, she might shut down.

"Boone, would you mind getting Phoebe a soda? I think she could use the sugar right now."

She watched as Boone shook off her emotions. "Sure, would you like that, Phoebe?"

"Uh-uh. You stay." She gripped Boone's hand fiercely. The tactic had worked, though, and Grey could see Boone focused more on how Phoebe was coping than on her own anger.

They were finally ushered back to see the doctor, with Grey accompanying them. Nothing was broken, thank goodness. They stitched up her upper lip but said her lower lip should heal fine. When it was time to leave, Grey turned to Phoebe.

"Do you have your own ride? Or would you like to ride with me?"

"Can't I ride with Boone?" Phoebe asked.

"I can follow you," Boone said.

"Sure. That's fine." Grey smiled inside at the idea of more time with Boone. She was impressed at Boone's willingness to help Phoebe through this. Often family members got so caught up in the anger and helplessness of the situation that they failed to give the victim what she needed most. The security of someone she trusted. Boone either understood this from experience or was intuitively sensitive to what was appropriate. Either way, she regretted judging her so quickly at the Chamber of Commerce mixer. She was obviously a deeply caring person.

"My car's that gray Lexus over there," Grey said. "Where are you?"

"Mine's the truck next to you," Boone said.

"Okay. I'll make sure you're behind me." Grey slid into her car.

She kept her eye on the rearview mirror and was relieved to see Boone behind her as they pulled through the security gates on the street.

They arrived at the shelter and Grey walked over to help Phoebe out of the truck. She guided them both inside the center.

"Welcome to Serene Pathway."

She showed them around the shared area, taking them to the kitchen, dining room, and den. She led them down the hallway where the counselors had their offices, and finally took them to Phoebe's room.

Boone looked around the room.

"This place is nice," she said.

Phoebe nodded.

"Do you have any belongings?" Grey asked.

"In my car," Phoebe mumbled.

"Oh, shit! Your car's still at the bar," Boone said.

"I'll take you to get it." Grey turned to Boone. "Unless you need to take off?"

Phoebe reached for Boone's hand.

"Please stay."

Boone looked down at her, a tender expression on her face.

"I'll hang around," Boone said. "But first we'll go get your car. You'll be okay until we get back."

They returned to the bar and Boone ran inside to let Christopher know she wouldn't be around for a while and

Grey waited for her by her car. When Boone came back out, Grey watched her climb behind the wheel of Phoebe's car and once again, they headed for the shelter.

Grey had Cecilia reschedule her day so she could spend as much of it with Boone and Phoebe as possible. She told herself Phoebe needed her, but she knew she wanted the time with Boone as well. There was something about her, a quiet strength that drew her to Boone. There was also that soft, caring side that Grey never would have guessed belonged to her. Either way, she was happy to spend her day with them.

"Is there anything I can get for you?" Grey asked Phoebe as she put her things away.

"You've done so much already," Phoebe whispered.

"I'm hoping to do so much more," Grey said. "With counseling and job training, we'll get you back on your feet in no time."

"How long can I stay?" Phoebe asked.

Grey had already gone over all that with her, but she knew residents were often in shock when she met them, so she patiently explained it again.

"You have a place here until you're ready to move on."

Phoebe nodded.

Grey saw Boone check her watch. Grey checked hers. It was already three o'clock.

"Will you be okay if I take off, Phoebs?" Boone asked.

Phoebe looked terrified. Pools of tears formed in her eyes.

"I can hang out if you want," Boone offered.

"No. It's okay. You'll stay with me?" Phoebe looked at Grey.

"Sure."

"Okay. You can go."

"I'll be back tomorrow to check on you," Boone said.

Grey felt her heart skip a beat. There was something about

Boone that intrigued her. Clearly, there was more to her than met the eye.

"I'll walk you out," Grey said. "Is that okay, Phoebe? I'll be right back."

Grey escorted Boone to her truck and gave her a security card so she'd be able to come see Phoebe whenever she wanted.

"You did the right thing you know, calling me."

"I'm so glad we bumped into each other the other night. I don't know what I would have done if I didn't know about your place."

"Well, you did, so it's all good. And we'll take good care of Phoebe."

"Thanks. I believe you."

Boone opened her door. Grey knew she wanted to see her again. Away from Phoebe and the shelter.

"Why don't we have dinner tonight?" Grey said.

"Tonight?"

"Yeah. We could both use it after this day, don't you think?"

"Yeah, we could."

"So, what do you say?"

Boone's eyes twinkled in merriment.

"Are you asking me on a date?"

"Not a date," Grey said, reminding herself what Boone did for a living. "I could never date you. But I am asking you to dinner."

"Sounds great. Where and when?"

"Say six o'clock? I can pick you up from the bar."

"I'd better not still be at the bar at six o'clock," Boone said. "How about I pick you up from here at six?"

"How about we meet at La Mirage at six?" Grey laughed. "Do you know where it is?"

"I do and I'll be there."

"Sounds great. See you then."

"Wait, Grey?"

"Yes?"

"Will Phoebe be okay then? Without you here?"

"I'll introduce one of the night staff to her. She'll be fine. I don't spend the night here, Boone."

Boone nodded her understanding.

"Right, then. See you tonight."

Boone drove off, her heart still heavy for Phoebe, but also a little lighter at the prospect of a date with Grey. Even though Grey said it wasn't a date. She hoped the night would end with Grey in her bed, date or not.

She pulled up at The Boonies and cringed at the sight of Tanner's truck there. She had to play it cool, act like she didn't know anything. It would be hard, since she wanted to rip his testicles off and shove them down his throat.

She walked in and went behind the bar to grab a beer and talk to Christopher.

"How'd today go?" she asked.

"No problem. I had it all under control. What was your big emergency?"

"Nothing I can talk about. Just some stuff I needed to deal with."

"You're okay, though?" Christopher asked.

"I'm just fine," Boone said.

"Hey, sis!" Tanner called to her.

"What's up, Tanner?" She wandered over, intent on playing it cool.

"You seen Phoebe today?"

"Phoebe? She doesn't usually come by here. You know that. She's not the barfly type."

"Don't bullshit me, Boone. I saw her car here earlier."

Boone felt her stomach clench.

"I don't know what to say. She wasn't here."

"Yeah? Well, how come I come in around the lunch rush and you're not here?" He sounded like he'd been there since the lunch rush, but she was sure she hadn't seen his truck when they'd picked up Phoebe's car.

"I had some personal stuff to attend to. No biggie. I can't be here twenty-four seven."

"Well, if you know where my wife is, you better tell me."

"What? Did you lose her or something? How the hell should I know where your wife is?"

"It's none of your fucking business why I'm asking. But I'm just sayin'."

"Fine. If I see her, I'll let her know you're looking for her."

"You'd better, if you know what's good for you. And her."

"Yes, sir." Her voice dripped with sarcasm. She was going to have another beer, but couldn't stand being around Tanner any longer.

"I'm out of here," she told Christopher. "I'll be back in the morning. Thanks again for today."

"No problem. I just hope everything's okay."

"It will be, Christopher. It will be."

She got home and quickly changed to swim a few laps to help ease the tension of the day. She took a shower and donned a pair of light gray slacks with a white button-down, short-sleeved shirt. She slipped on black loafers and grabbed her keys. She'd make it a little early, but that was better than being late.

She needn't have worried about being early. She parked right next to Grey's Lexus and walked in to find Grey already seated at a table for two.

"I thought I'd be early," Boone said.

"I'm always early," Grey said. "Better than being late."

"I agree."

"Have you ordered anything yet?" Boone asked.

"No. I was waiting for you. I thought about ordering a bottle of wine, but thought since you're in the business, you may have a better idea of what's good."

Boone blushed at the compliment.

"I don't know a lot about wine, but I'll give it my best shot."

She ordered a nice bottle of Malbec, which they sipped while perusing their menus. They placed their orders and Boone found herself nervous as a schoolgirl. She told herself to pull it together and make conversation.

"So, wow. That's a tough business you're in," she finally said.

"It has its moments."

"Are all cases as bad as Phoebe?"

"Some better, some worse."

"I'm sorry. Would you rather not talk about work when you're off the clock?"

"I'm never completely off the clock, and I'm fine talking about it. I'm very passionate about what I do."

"I can tell. I really admire that about you." She felt awkward, so quickly added, "I really appreciate all you did for Phoebe today."

"Well, I can tell she appreciated you, too, Boone. You were very good with her."

"I was just happy to be able to help her. I could kill my brother for what he did."

"I was a little surprised that she came to you, what with you being the abuser's sister and all."

"I was, too. But I'm glad she did."

"What do you think your brother's going to do? Will he try to find her?"

"Does that happen often? Do they find women at your place?"

"Never. I've never had that happen. Don't worry, Boone. Phoebe is safe with us."

"My brother was pretty pissed off," Boone said.

"You mean when he did that to her?"

"No. I mean he was at the bar when I got back this afternoon. He'd seen her car there and thinks I know where she is."

"I hope you denied it."

"I will 'til my dying day."

They ate their dinner, keeping up a constant flow of conversation.

"So, where'd you go to school, Grey?"

"Oregon State. You?"

Boone laughed out loud. Of course.

"U of O."

Grey laughed, too.

"So we're sworn enemies, huh?" Grey joked.

"After our first meeting, one might have thought so."

"I suppose I owe you an apology for that," Grey said.

"No. I get it now. And it scares me. I wish I could do more to help."

"You can. Get involved. Or at least post signs in your bar. Not now, of course. That would be too obvious to Phoebe's husband and he might get violent with you."

"Let him try," Boone said.

Dinner was finished and Boone took out her credit card.

"Put that away," Grey said.

"What? Why?"

"I asked you out, remember? This is my treat."

"Actually, the treat has been mine," Boone said.

"Aw. Thank you. But I do insist on getting the bill."

"I'll get it next time," Boone said without thinking.

Grey looked at her, but said nothing.

They walked out to their cars and Boone didn't want the evening to end.

"Thank you for tonight. That was really nice," she said.

"Thank you."

They stood in the parking lot in silence and Boone couldn't resist. She pulled Grey to her and hugged her tight. The hug lasted longer than she'd anticipated, but she didn't mind. Soon, she was stroking Grey's back and caught herself, knowing she needed to keep things in check.

She turned to kiss Grey's cheek, but Grey turned her head slightly and their lips met. It was brief, but wonderful. Boone felt her heart race and forced herself to stand up straight.

"Can I call you?" she asked.

"I don't think that would be a good idea," Grey said.

"When are you going to realize I'm not a monster just because I own a bar? Tell me you didn't have a good time this evening."

"I did, Boone. I had a wonderful time. But it doesn't change the fact that what you do contributes to everything I'm against."

"But I'm not an abusive type. And neither are my patrons."

"You don't know that."

Boone was frustrated. It wasn't fair for Grey to judge her because of her line of work. What was she thinking anyway? Grey wasn't going to be up for a quick tumble in the sheets. That much was clear. Anything more wasn't worth the effort.

"Well, will I see you tomorrow when I go visit Phoebe?"

"Maybe. I might be busy. I do have to see clients tomorrow."

"Okay. Well, I'll be there."

"I'll probably see you then."

CHAPTER SEVEN

Grey arrived at the shelter the next morning, and the first thing she did was check in with her night help to see how Phoebe had fared. She learned that she had spent most of the night in her room, only coming out to use the facilities. Grey made her way down the hall to her room and knocked on the door. She heard muffled cries from within.

"Phoebe, honey, it's Grey. Can I come in?"

The door opened and Phoebe stood there, still in the same clothes from the day before, looking rumpled and much the worse for wear.

"Good morning. Did you sleep last night?"

"A little."

"Would you like some breakfast? Some coffee maybe?"

"It would hurt."

"Honey, you have to eat something. You have to take care of yourself. And let us help with that. Why don't you go take a shower, then I'll take you to the kitchen and we'll find something for you to eat."

Phoebe padded down the hall to the showers, and Grey went to her office to check her messages. She listened to them and jotted notes in her computer. She tried to focus, but kept flashing back to the brief kiss the night before. It had been so tender and so sweet and she wanted more. She hated admitting that to herself. Boone Fairway was not going to happen. End of story.

She made her way back to Phoebe's room and got there just as Phoebe was coming down the hall in her bathrobe.

"Okay. Doesn't that feel better?"

Phoebe nodded.

"Now you get dressed. I'm going to my office. Do you remember where that is?"

Phoebe nodded again.

"Good. After you're dressed, come find me and I'll show you to the kitchen before I start my day."

She was working on paperwork when Phoebe appeared in the door, dressed in a fresh pair of shorts and a T-shirt.

"You look very comfortable. Let's get you some food and I'll take you as my first appointment today, okay?"

She watched Phoebe grimace as she ate some oatmeal and drank some coffee. Grey was sure it had to hurt, but she also knew Phoebe needed nourishment. When she was finished, Grey led her to her office.

"Go ahead and have a seat on the couch." Grey closed the door behind her. "Let's talk about your relationship with your husband. Has he ever been abusive to you before?"

Phoebe looked at her shoes and nodded.

"It's nothing to be ashamed of," Grey said. "It happens to many women. Men, too."

"I should be like Boone. I'll never be with another man," Phoebe said.

"It happens to lesbians, too, Phoebe. And gay men. No one is immune. You're not alone."

Phoebe just stared at her, seeming not to comprehend what she was hearing.

"You're kidding, right?"

"No, violence and abuse is universal, Phoebe. We are all at risk. It's something we have to educate people about. No one deserves to be battered or verbally abused. You're one of many, Phoebe. Do you want to tell me how long this has been going on?"

"It started almost immediately after we got married. Nine years ago."

"That's a long time to put up with it," Grey said softly.

Phoebe nodded.

"So, are you convinced this time that you're through with the abuse?"

"I am."

"Good. I would prefer you not go back to him."

"I can't. He's going to be madder that I left him. Imagine what he'd do to me now." She visibly shuddered.

Grey was pleased at the long answer she had gotten from Phoebe. It was a good sign.

"Do you have a job?" Grey asked.

Phoebe shook her head.

"Have you ever had a job?"

"I worked for my dad in high school."

"Doing what?"

"I kept the books for his lumber yard."

"Oh, good. That's great that you have a skill set. We have a job counselor here who can help you find a job so you can support yourself."

"Can't I get alimony?"

"That's something we can discuss. We also have legal volunteers who come in to help women with that. Are you sure you want to divorce him?"

"Yes."

"Good. Hold on to that thought." She knew women often felt that way when they first arrived at the shelter, but changed their minds later on.

They went on with their session and Phoebe agreed to meet with Connie to discuss job options.

"I'll check on you later today and I want another session with you tomorrow, okay?"

"Okay."

❖

Boone got through her morning work on autopilot; her mind was on Grey Dawson and Phoebe. She wanted to get out of the bar as soon as she could to go see how Phoebe was doing. And she couldn't lie to herself; she hoped to run into Grey as well. She was a pain in her ass, but the kiss they'd shared said something more could happen. And Boone wanted something to happen with Grey. Just one night and she'd be happy. She planned to make that happen.

When the lunch rush was over, she helped clean up, then left the bar in the capable hands of her staff. She drove over to Serene Pathway and showed her card to the guard at the gate. She parked and knocked on the door. It was answered by a short, gray-haired woman.

"Can I help you?" the woman asked.

"Hi. I'm Boone. I'm Phoebe's sister-in-law. I don't know the rules on visiting."

"You're welcome to visit, Boone. I'm Cecilia. I'm Grey's right-hand woman. Come on in. Would you like me to go get Phoebe for you or at least let her know you're here?"

"I know where her room is. I don't mind walking down there."

"I'll take you," Cecilia said.

She led Boone down the halls to Phoebe's room. Boone tried not to look around too much, as she wanted to afford the other residents their privacy, but she really hoped to catch a glimpse of Grey.

When Phoebe opened her door, Boone had to tamp down her reaction. The bruises looked worse than they had the day before.

She turned quickly to Cecilia then regrouped and focused on Phoebe.

"How are you doing, today, Phoebs?"

Phoebe shrugged.

"You still hurt, I bet, huh?"

"Yeah."

They sat on the couch.

"I'm so sorry, Phoebe. I hope you know how sorry I am."

"I do." She was silent for a while, then looked Boone in the eye. "Have you seen him?"

"I ran into him yesterday."

Phoebe nodded. Boone was unsure of what to say. She probably should have gone over this with Grey the night before. How much was she supposed to share?

"Did he say anything?"

"He didn't tell me what happened, if that's what you mean."

"What did he say?"

"He'd seen your car at the bar yesterday, so he thought I knew where you were."

Phoebe's eyes grew wide.

"What did you tell him?"

"I told him I hadn't seen you."

"Was he pissed?"

"Yeah," Boone said. "He was pretty hot."

"He scares me when he gets like that."

"Well, you don't ever have to worry about that again." When Phoebe didn't say anything, she said, "Right?"

"Right." Phoebe stared out the window for a moment. "Will he find me, Boone? Can he get to me here?"

Boone took Phoebe's hands in hers and looked her square in the eye.

"No, Phoebe. Absolutely not. You're totally safe here. Will you promise me you'll relax and allow yourself to be cared for?"

"I'm scared," Phoebe whispered.

"Don't be. You're safe. I promise you. Grey won't let anything happen to you here."

"I heard my name," Grey said from the door. "What did I miss?"

Boone stood, taking in the professional Grey who had walked up unnoticed. Grey looked sharp in her business suit. Almost as nice as she had in her blue dress the night before, only in a different, more professional way. Suddenly, it was hard to find her voice.

"I was just reassuring Phoebe that she's safe here," Boone finally said.

"Yes, Phoebe. You're very safe here. Boone, please sit back down. I didn't mean to interrupt. I was just coming to check on Phoebe, but I see she's in good hands."

"Still, you're welcome to join us." Boone wanted to spend more time with Grey. She felt like a heel, but reminded herself she really did care for Phoebe and would be there even if Grey wasn't.

"Maybe for a few minutes." Grey sat in the wingback chair and crossed her shapely legs. Boone wanted to kiss her, starting at her ankles before moving up to other parts. She shook the thought from her head.

"So, Phoebe," Grey said. "What are you most worried about?"

"I don't want him to find me," Phoebe said quietly.

"Your husband? Oh, he won't. We're very secretive in our location. We're unlisted and closely guarded. This is an extremely safe place. Please don't worry."

Boone saw the tears in Phoebe's eyes and wished there was something she could do to help ease the fear. But she guessed it was only natural after what Phoebe had been through. Boone hated her brother more than ever. How dare he lay a hand on sweet Phoebe, who would never hurt anybody?

"Boone? Are you with us?" Grey's voice broke through her thoughts.

"I'm sorry. What were you saying?"

"We were talking about how you'll always be here for Phoebe and she needs to learn to trust you and me and then we'll work on her trusting other people."

"Right," Boone said. "I'm sure that'll be a hard lesson to learn, but we're here for you and that's a start."

"I trust you, Boone," Phoebe said. "I do."

"I'm glad. You need to trust Grey, too, though."

"I'll try."

"Good." She stood. "Now, it's time for me to get going. Is there anything you need me to bring you tomorrow when I come by?"

Phoebe shook her head.

Grey stood as well.

"I'll walk you out."

"So, tell me," Boone said when they were out of earshot. "How's she doing? I have nothing to compare this to, so I'm kind of freaking out."

"She's doing okay. She needed to be reminded to shower

and eat this morning. But that's not unusual. This will be a long process, Boone. And it's just started. She's got a long road ahead of her. It's nice that she has you to help keep her positive."

"She asked me about Tanner," Boone said. "I wasn't sure what to say."

"Be honest. Always be honest. She needs to be able to trust you, like we were saying."

Boone nodded as they arrived at her truck. She shifted her weight from one foot to the other, wanting desperately to ask Grey out, but not wanting to appear desperate. She decided to bite the bullet.

"I'd like to see you again," she said.

"I thought we covered this last night."

"Look, I'm not asking you to marry me or anything. I just thought another dinner would be nice."

"I realize this. But I don't want to lead you on or give you any false hope. There's no chance of anything happening between us."

"You've made that perfectly clear. Let's just say I want to thank you for helping Phoebe."

"It's my job, Boone."

"I get that."

There was an awkward silence.

"So, no chance of dinner?"

"I suppose one more dinner wouldn't hurt. But that's it. Just one more."

"Really?"

"Really," Grey said.

"Great. I'll look forward to it."

"Don't get your hopes up too high."

"How could I? Where shall we meet?"

"Why don't you pick me up at my place?"

"Sounds great. Where do you live?"

She told Boone her address. "Do you need me to write that down?"

"I got it." Boone opened her glove compartment and wrote down the address.

"Great. What time will you pick me up?"

"Six o'clock again?"

"Sounds great. I'll see you then."

❖

Grey finished up her day with an anxious stomach. She couldn't wait to see Boone again, socially, but she was nervous about her feelings. She didn't usually feel such a strong attraction to a woman immediately. Yet there was something about Boone that drew her to her. At first, sure, she was attracted to her physically. Who wouldn't be? But now she could see there was more to her. She was caring, compassionate, intelligent. All traits Grey admired. She had to admit to herself she was really looking forward to getting to know Boone better. Although she knew better than to allow herself to get too close. Because Boone was off-limits in a big way. Looks and everything else aside, Boone was the wrong woman for Grey to be looking at. Still, she couldn't deny the physical need that overcame her every time she thought of her.

She got home and took a quick shower to freshen up. She dressed in a red peasant skirt and yellow blouse, knowing bright summer colors wouldn't be appropriate much longer. She applied light makeup, eyeliner, blush, and lip gloss and called it good. She was ready with fifteen minutes to spare and had nothing to do those last minutes but feel the butterflies in her stomach.

Boone showed up five minutes early, looking dapper

in chinos and a blue golf shirt. She smelled good, too. Her cologne was soft and sensual, and Grey knew she could nuzzle that neck and inhale it all night if things were different.

"You look great," Boone said, openly admiring Grey's attire.

"Thanks, so do you." Grey wanted to tell her she looked and smelled delicious, but fought the urge.

"I hope you like Mexican?" Boone said.

"I love Mexican."

"Good, because I'm jonesin' for a really good margarita, and I know just where to get one."

"Sounds good to me," Grey said.

They arrived at the restaurant and each ordered a Cadillac margarita. They were relaxing and enjoying each other's company, and Grey felt her insides melt every time she looked into Boone's eyes. She felt like her body was betraying her. She fought to maintain her professional decorum.

"So how was the rest of your day?" Boone asked.

"Uneventful. And yours?"

"Nice. Tanner didn't show up at the bar this afternoon, so that was a good thing."

Grey was sorry Boone had had to experience the ugliness that was domestic abuse, but she was glad they at least had some common ground now.

"That's good. You know, if I haven't emphasized it enough, I'm really glad you came to visit Phoebe today. It's nice for these women to know they're not alone in the world. So many of the women feel completely disconnected."

"I'd hate for Phoebe to think she lost her family. Just one ugly member of it, and that's no great loss."

They sat in silence for a few moments as they munched on chips and salsa.

"So, how did you get into the business you're in?" Boone asked.

"That's an awfully personal subject."

"I'm sorry. I didn't know."

"Well, I suppose it's fair for you to know."

"Only if you want to share," Boone said.

"My father hung out in bars when I was a kid."

"Oh, no. This isn't going to be good."

"He'd come home in a foul mood every night. Drunk as a skunk."

"Grey, I'm so sorry."

"And he'd take out his anger on anyone. My mom was his favorite target, of course, but kids weren't above it."

"I don't know what to say."

"I was his favorite, so I didn't get as much as the others, but I got my fair share. And even when I wasn't being beaten, I had to watch my mother and siblings taking it from him. That's why I went into domestic abuse counseling and finally opened Serene Pathway."

"I'm so sorry," Boone said again.

"It's not something many people fully understand."

"My father was the same way," Boone said. "Obviously, in Tanner, the apple didn't fall far from the tree."

"I'm sorry for you, too, Boone."

"Yeah, since I've met you I've spent a lot of time wishing I'd known of places like yours for my mother back in the day."

"They weren't as prolific back then. Women were supposed to stay with their husbands, no matter what."

"A lot of women still feel that way," Boone said.

"What led you to open a bar then? With that history? And now with your brother? It seems like a bar would be the last business you would want to own."

"I told you. My bar isn't like other bars. It's a social gathering place. People don't get sloshed and go beat up their spouses or partners."

"But you don't know that."

"But I think I do."

"But you can't. But still, you haven't answered the original question. Why a bar?"

"I saw a need for a sports bar in the neighborhood and thought I may as well be the one to open it. It was strictly a business decision in the beginning."

"And now?"

"Now it's my pride and joy."

"So you see why I can't be in a relationship with you, Boone."

"Not really. I know now that we have more in common than either of us thought. But again, like I said, I'm not asking for a relationship anyway."

"You probably have your choice of women at the bar," Grey said, not really wanting to hear the answer.

"I'm not sure exactly how to answer that."

"Honestly."

"There are always women at the bar."

Grey felt her heart sink. She felt like her body was betraying her mind. She found herself wanting Boone desperately, but knew it could never happen.

"Now, on to lighter subjects," Boone finally said. "Being a Beaver, do you follow your team? Or are sports not your thing?"

"I'm not a die-hard or anything, but I do try to listen to the games on the radio if I'm home."

"What about other sports?"

Grey laughed outwardly, while cringing inwardly, hoping she wouldn't be judged.

"I'm not a big sportsaholic, if that's what you're asking."

"Maybe not, but I'd love it if you'd come to the bar with me to watch a game sometime."

Grey pondered the offer. A sports bar was not someplace she really ever saw herself, for many reasons, not the least of which being the abuse factor. But if it meant more time with Boone… She shook her head, unwilling to consider it.

"I don't think that would be a good idea," Grey said.

"Why not? I mean, I know you're not big on sports bars and all, but I'd like you to experience where I work since I've experienced where you do. And I'd like you to see it's not the den of iniquity you seem to picture it as."

"I don't think I can put aside my prejudice and be open-minded. Not even once."

"That's too bad," Boone said. "I really think it would be a good experience for you."

Grey pondered what Boone was saying. Would it be a good experience? How could it be? It was against everything she believed in. But it was intriguing to think of seeing Boone in her environment. She thought it must be the margarita going to her head. She wasn't thinking clearly to even consider it.

"Convince me."

"You could come with me, watch a little football, see the crowd of nice people, and feel better about having expanded your horizons."

"I suppose one trip wouldn't hurt."

"So it's a date."

"Sure, why not?"

"Really? It's a date?"

"Sure. Just because I don't like what you do doesn't mean I don't like you."

The words were out before she could stop them. She regretted saying them in the silence that followed.

Boone stared at her and finally smiled. "Great. Because I really like you."

Grey's heart thumped in her chest. She couldn't believe she'd said that out loud. She felt like she needed to clarify. "But know I don't believe there's any chance of anything happening between us."

"Nothing?" Boone smiled.

Grey blushed deeply. She desperately wanted something to happen, and that was so out of character for her. But she wanted Boone Fairway. She just hoped she could keep her hormones in check. She knew there could never be a future between the two of them, and she felt it would be unfair to lead Boone on. But she wasn't sure she could control herself.

After dinner, they climbed back into Boone's truck. Grey was a nervous wreck. She wanted Boone so badly, but didn't want to push too hard or appear too easy. She vowed to let Boone set the pace for them.

"What's on your mind?" Boone asked.

"Just thinking how nice the past two evenings have been."

"They really have been. I enjoy your company, Grey."

"Thank you. I enjoy yours, too."

They reached Grey's house, and Boone walked her to the door.

"Would you like to come in for another drink?" Grey was hesitant to ask, but longed to prolong the evening.

"That would be great. Thanks."

Grey led Boone inside and showed her to the living room, where Boone took a seat on the brown leather couch. Grey was proud of her house, painted in soothing earth tones.

"I like your place," Boone said.

"Thank you," Grey called from the dining area where she was pouring Boone a bourbon and herself a glass of white wine.

She returned to the living room and sat on the couch with Boone, far enough away not to appear obvious.

"So, tell me your deepest, darkest secret," Boone said.

Grey felt the blush creep up her chest to cover her face. Her secret was she wanted Boone and wanted her now. She wasn't about to say that. The blush must not have escaped Boone as she arched an eyebrow.

"That good, huh?" Boone said.

Grey blushed harder and laughed.

"No. I don't really have a deep, dark secret."

"I don't know if I believe you. What happened to that trust?" Boone teased her and leaned closer. She reached out a hand and ran her fingers through the ends of Grey's hair.

Grey felt her nipples harden at the light touch. She hoped they didn't show through her blouse. She was more excited than she had been in years, and she would do anything to have Boone.

"Okay. So my secret is I like you. A lot. Even though I shouldn't."

"That's a great secret," Boone said. "I like you, too."

"I feel like a silly schoolgirl," Grey said.

"You're not, though. You're a grown woman." Boone's face was now within inches of hers and Grey felt her breath catch. She felt the heat radiating from Boone, smelled the rugged scent of her cologne. She watched as if in slow motion as Boone's mouth moved closer to hers. She closed her eyes as their lips met.

Her head grew light and her heart leapt as they kissed. It wasn't a long kiss, but the need was apparent in it. She felt her thighs dampen.

Boone pulled away and set her drink on the coffee table.

"That was nice," she said.

"Yes, it was." Grey wanted to shout that it was amazing, the best kiss she'd ever had.

Boone took Grey's glass and set it next to hers. She leaned over again, this time with her hand behind Grey's head. Grey was about to burst and their lips hadn't even met again yet.

Grey felt Boone's lips on hers and opened her mouth, welcoming Boone's tongue inside. The kiss was powerful and intense. She wrapped her arms around Boone's broad shoulders and held on while the kiss deepened.

Grey was lost in the sea of sensations that flooded her body. Boone was an excellent kisser, and she never wanted the moment to end. She leaned back on the couch, pulling Boone on top of her. She opened her legs and felt Boone's leg slip between hers.

Boone was grinding into her and Grey thought she'd surely lose control any minute. She was certain she'd come fully clothed. She pulled Boone closer and was rewarded with a deeper kiss.

Finally, Boone broke the kiss and sat up, pulling Grey with her. Grey was light-headed and breathing heavily. Thankfully, Boone seemed to be having a hard time catching her breath as well.

"I'm sorry," Boone said. "I don't know what got into me."

Grey was crushed. And embarrassed. There was no need to apologize. She decided to be brave and call Boone on it.

"You're sorry? Is that an honest statement?"

Boone stared at her.

"No. No, it's not. But yes, it is. I'm sorry to try to push too hard too fast. But I'm not sorry I kissed you like that. It was wonderful."

"Okay. Well, no apologies necessary, Boone. I'm a big girl and I'll let you know if things are at a pace I'm not comfortable with, okay? Honesty and trust, Boone. You've got to trust me."

Boone nodded.

"You're right. So we're okay?"

"We're fantastic," Grey said, then blushed again.

"I should get going," Boone said.

"Is that what you want?" Grey grew bolder by the moment. Her hormones seemed to have taken control of her mouth. Her brain kicked into gear then. "You're right, of course. You should go."

"It's what I think would be best, too. We'll leave it at this for now."

"Okay, I agree."

"Good."

They walked out to Boone's truck. She pulled Grey to her and kissed her again. Grey felt her knees grow weak.

When the kiss ended, Boone said, "I'll see you tomorrow."

"I'm looking forward to it."

"Me, too."

Chapter Eight

Boone drove back to Serene Pathway the next day filled with trepidation. Sure, Grey had said the make-out session the night before was fine, but she still felt she lost control, and she knew Grey was still hesitant about her. Although, Grey had a point, too. She was a grown woman and could say stop whenever she wanted.

There was something about Grey, though. Boone felt like maybe there could be more. She didn't know if it was Grey's professionalism, her sense of humor, or what, but Boone felt like she wanted to see how far she could go with her. And not sexually. This was uncharted territory for her. Her gut instinct was to take it slow. Wasn't that the rule? But damn, she wanted Grey Dawson!

She pulled up at the shelter and knocked on the door. She was led to the office by Cecilia and stopped short when she saw Grey seated at her desk. She was facing away from Boone, but turned when the door closed.

"Hi, Grey."

Grey stood and kissed her on the cheek.

"Hi, Boone. You'll be happy to know Phoebe is doing better today."

"Really? That's great. How so?"

"She took a shower without being reminded and helped

out in the kitchen serving lunch today. Socializing with the others is a very good sign."

"It means she's not afraid of the whole world, right?"

"Right. Although it's a far cry from being okay with the outside world, it's nice to know she's comfortable around other survivors."

"That's great," Boone said, happy for a topic of conversation not related to the previous night's events. She was very impressed with Grey. The light kiss on the cheek showed that she thought of her as more than just another visitor, but the conversation showed she could keep it professional when the situation dictated. Yet another plus for Grey Dawson.

"She's in the living area now, if you want to go see her."

"Thanks, I'll do just that."

"Oh, and, Boone?"

"Yeah?"

"Tonight's my treat."

"Again tonight, huh?" Boone's heart soared.

"Is that okay?"

"It's great. I'll pick you up at six again."

"Sounds wonderful. Only I'll be cooking, so you won't be picking me up. Just come hungry."

Boone doubted her hunger for Grey could be much more apparent than it had been.

"I'll be hungry, all right."

She walked down the hall and found Phoebe watching television with a couple of other women.

She sat on the couch next to her.

"How you doing, Phoebs?"

"I'm okay."

"You look good." It wasn't a complete lie. Her face still looked horrible, but her eyes weren't filled with the fear of the past couple of days.

Phoebe smiled.

"I look a mess."

"Not true. Your lips even look like the swelling's gone down."

"I guess."

"So, how's today been? Better?"

"I guess."

"How are you feeling, Phoebs? Be honest."

"I'm tired, Boone. I'm exhausted. I just want to lie in my bed and cry."

"Why don't you do that?"

"The tears hurt my cuts."

Boone nodded.

"And I have to live. If I don't, he wins."

"Good attitude. I like that. You do have to live. You'll come out of this stronger, better. Trust me."

"I'll come out of this a lesbian or a nun. Except Grey says lesbians hurt each other, too. Did you know that?"

"I guess I never really thought about that."

"So I guess I'll be a nun."

Boone pulled Phoebe close and held her.

"No, sweetheart. You'll find someone who really loves the sweet and wonderful person you are and who'd never dream of doing this to you."

Phoebe pulled away.

"I don't know. If I made Tanner this mad, I could make somebody else this mad, too."

"Phoebe, this wasn't your fault." She was careful not to raise her voice. "Please don't ever think that. Tanner's got a screw loose to do this to you. You didn't do anything wrong."

Phoebe's bottom lip trembled.

"But I made him mad. I never should have made him mad."

"What he did was inexcusable. Men don't hit women. Hell, people don't hit other people just because they're mad. It's just not done. You couldn't prevent this from happening, Phoebs. Trust me."

"Trust. There's that word again."

"It's important. And you need to trust me and Grey when we tell you this wasn't your fault."

"I'll try."

"Good girl. Okay. I'm gonna head out now. You have fun with your friends and I'll see you tomorrow, okay?"

"What day's tomorrow?"

"It's Saturday. Why?"

"You don't have to come out here on your weekend."

"Phoebe, I love you. I want to come see you."

"Will Grey be here tomorrow?"

"I honestly don't know. You should ask her."

"If she's not here, I'll be really glad if you come."

"I will, Phoebs. I promise. I'll see you tomorrow."

She drove back to the bar and grabbed a beer. It was a jumpin' Friday afternoon, and happy hour was in full swing. She sat on a bar stool to watch the Mariners playing the Yankees. The Mariners were losing. How appropriate.

"You haven't been around much the past couple of days." Dani sidled up next to her.

"No, I've been pretty busy. How you doing?"

"You weren't even here last night for the football game. What's up with that?"

"I had things going on. I know. It was weird not to be here, but life goes on."

"Well, you'll be here for the Ducks game tomorrow, won't you?"

"I sure plan on it." Boone hoped to bring Grey to the Ducks game, but didn't want to share that with Dani.

"Good. I'll see you there. You want to shoot some pool or something now?"

Boone couldn't explain it, but she felt guilty even talking to Dani. She told herself she was being ridiculous. Grey had made it perfectly clear there was nothing between them. But then last night had happened…

"I'm not really feeling it right now. Sorry. I just kind of want to watch the game."

"Was it something I said? Did I do something wrong?"

"Not at all. I'm just not up for much right now."

"You feelin' okay?"

"I've just got a lot going on. No worries."

"Okay. Well, if you need to talk, I'm around."

"Thanks, Dani."

Boone had another beer and pondered what might be ahead for her that evening. She didn't know if she'd be strong enough to pull back in the heat of passion. She remembered Grey's words and her own about trust. She had to trust Grey. And she did.

She finished her beer then left for home to get ready for her date. She was excited at the prospect of Grey cooking for her. She wondered what she should wear. A dinner at a lady's house was different from a dinner at a restaurant. But how much more casual should she go? She was actually nervous, worried about making sure everything was just right.

She finally decided on a pair of cargo pants and a purple short-sleeved shirt. She looked nice but casual. That should work. She hoped she was neither over- nor underdressed and had to laugh at herself for being such a case about it.

Boone stopped by the florist shop on her way over to Grey's and picked a nice autumn bouquet for her. She hoped it would work, but figured the orange flowers would go well in Grey's house.

She arrived just before six and knocked on the door.

Grey opened it wearing blue capris and a print blue shirt. She looked beautiful.

"You look amazing." Boone bent to kiss her cheek.

"So do you. And those flowers are gorgeous. How did you know chrysanthemums were my favorite?"

"Lucky guess." Boone smiled.

"Come on in. I hope you don't mind, but I planned on putting you to work this evening."

"How so?"

"I've got everything ready except the steaks. I thought you might know your way around a grill better than I do."

"I do know how to grill," Boone said. She let Grey lead her to the backyard, admiring the sway of her hips as they went.

"Here's the grill. I'm completely clueless about how to work it," Grey admitted.

Boone fired it up, then went inside to get the steaks. Their conversation was light as she grilled, and when she removed the steaks, they were cooked to perfection.

They sat at Grey's dining room table with the flowers as a centerpiece. Grey poured their wine and brought out the side dishes. Boone served, her stomach growling at the aromas around her.

"How was your day?" Boone asked.

"It was good. As you saw, I even had time to catch up on paperwork. Not bad. How was yours?"

"It was really good. I stopped by the bar on my way home and it was jumpin'. That always makes me happy."

"So when did you want to take me there?" Grey asked.

"Where? Oh, the bar? How about for the Ducks game tomorrow night? Would it kill you to pretend to like the Ducks?" She laughed.

"I think I could do that. I actually think I'd like to see your bar. Will I be overwhelmed?"

"Maybe. But I hope you'll just have fun. Just don't wear Beaver colors, okay?"

"You've got it. I won't. I just hope I'll be able to relax in that environment."

"Any time you're not, you just say the word and I'll take you home."

They finished dinner and Boone helped Grey clear the table. Grey had already cleaned the kitchen, so there was only their dinner dishes and serving dishes to wash. They worked well together. Boone cleared and put dishes in the sink and dried. Grey washed.

Boone slid another dish around Grey and into the sink. Grey turned around to face her, trapping herself between Boone and the sink. Boone instinctively wrapped her arms around Grey.

"Hi there." She smiled.

"Hi, yourself," Grey said. "I kind of like your arms around me."

"Yeah? It kind of works for me, too."

Grey slid her arms around Boone's neck and pulled her close.

Boone followed her instincts and bent to kiss Grey lightly on the lips.

"That was nice," Grey said.

Boone kissed her neck and jaw, pausing to suck an earlobe before kissing her again. She tasted amazing. Every inch of her tasted clean and fresh. She didn't know what perfume she wore, but it was light and tantalizing but not overwhelming.

Grey opened her mouth and Boone let her tongue languidly wander in, tasting the warm red wine they'd shared.

She felt Grey's grip tighten and moved as close as she

could, feeling the heat of Grey against her. She forced herself to keep her hands behind Grey's back, lest she be tempted to let them wander too far.

Boone needn't have worried. Grey reached behind herself and grabbed Boone's hands, moving them firmly to her breasts.

"Oh, God," Boone breathed. Grey's breasts were small but pert, and they reacted immediately to Boone's touch. She felt the nipples poking through the flimsy material of her blouse.

She wanted more. She longed to take the nipples in her mouth, to lay Grey bare and have her way with her.

Grey pulled away and led Boone to the living room. She lay on the couch and pulled Boone on top of her. Boone loved the way their bodies fit together. She wasn't sure how far Grey would let her go, but she was certainly determined to find out.

They resumed kissing and Boone slipped her hand inside Grey's blouse to fondle her breasts over her silky bra. She deftly pushed one cup up and freed a breast; her crotch spasmed as she felt the soft flesh and hard nipple against her hand.

They continued to kiss, tongues wrapped around each other while Boone continued to explore under Grey's top. She finally let her hand slip down Grey's soft belly to tease her under her waistband.

Grey responded by arching her hips, urging Boone on. Boone moved her mouth away from Grey's and kissed her neck and ear before claiming her mouth again. She was lost in the moment, caught up in the passion she was feeling. She needed Grey. She needed all of her and wasn't sure how she'd stop if Grey said to. That thought made her stop cold.

She held herself up on her hands and looked into Grey's eyes.

"Are you okay?" she asked.

"Never better."

"You sure?"

"I'm positive," Grey said. "I told you. I'm a big girl."

Boone needed nothing else. She kissed Grey again as her hand fumbled with the button on her capris. She got it undone and unzipped the pants, sliding her hand inside. She teased herself by rubbing Grey's belly briefly before slipping her hand lower to feel the wet crotch of her panties. She rubbed her over it, feeling her hard clit underneath.

"Let's go to my room." Grey was breathing heavily, and Boone knew she was on the right track.

"Okay." Boone stood and helped Grey off the couch.

Grey stepped out of her capris and led Boone down the hall to her bedroom. Once there, Grey stripped out of the rest of her clothes and Boone did the same with hers. She took in the sight of Grey's naked body and held her breath for a moment.

"Do you have any idea how beautiful you are?" Boone said.

Grey reached out her hand and pulled Boone onto the bed with her. They lay tangled together, breasts pressed together, legs entwined, and kissed for what seemed like hours. Boone relished the feel of Grey's body against hers.

Finally, Boone kissed down Grey's neck and chest and licked a hard nipple. She licked it once, twice, just listening to Grey's reaction before she took it in her mouth. She ran her tongue over it and sucked on it while she moved her hand down Grey's body.

Grey opened her legs for Boone, who ran her fingers along the length of her. She was hot and slick and inviting. Boone circled Grey's swollen clit with her fingers, making Grey arch and thrust, trying to get contact. Boone finally pressed her fingers on it and rubbed as fast as she could. Grey screamed out in pleasure and Boone continued until Grey had settled down.

Far from finished, Boone slipped her fingers inside Grey and caressed her satin walls. She plunged her fingers in and out, coaxing Grey closer and closer until Grey finally arched her back, frozen in the climax that overcame her.

Boone continued until Grey begged her to stop.

"Please, I can't take any more."

"Are you sure?" Boone grinned.

"I'm positive. I can't. You need to stop."

"Mm. Okay. If you're sure." She dragged her fingers along the length of Grey again and moved her hand up until she could wrap her arm around her waist. She pulled her close and held her.

"Oh, no," Grey said. "You're not falling asleep now."

"No?" Boone said.

"No way."

Grey rolled Boone over and nibbled her breast. She licked and nipped it briefly before she suckled Boone's nipple. Boone groaned her appreciation and Grey tugged one last time before kissing down Boone's taut belly. She spread her legs and drew in a deep breath.

"You smell amazing," Grey said.

Boone was thankful she couldn't see her blush from that angle. She felt Grey's tongue on her and caught her breath. Grey knew what she was doing. There was no doubt. She had Boone writhing, begging for more. Boone felt her tongue dip inside her and knew she wouldn't be able to hold on much longer. She licked across her clit and Boone felt her stomach tighten and release as the orgasm washed over her.

Boone lay on her back and Grey curled next to her, resting her head on her shoulder.

"Now am I allowed to go to sleep?" Boone laughed.

"Are you always such a romantic?" Grey laughed as well.

"Mm. That was wonderful, Grey. You're an amazing lover."

"You're not so bad yourself."

"We're good together. I guess we should have known we would be."

"Why's that?"

"The chemistry between us." Boone wondered if she'd said too much. She figured, what the hell, she'd started it, may as well finish it. "Or am I the only one who feels that?"

"Oh, no. You're definitely not the only one who feels it. It's intense, isn't it?"

"It really is. I really like you, Grey."

"I like you, too, Boone."

"So, can we do this again?" Boone asked.

"What? Right now? Because I don't think I can take any more right now."

"No. Not right now. You know what I mean."

"I do know what you mean. And I'd like very much to do this with you again. And again. And again, if you want to know the truth."

"I think I always want to know the truth with you, Grey."

"I'd like the same from you."

"You got it." Boone kissed the top of her head.

❖

Grey woke the next morning and a slow smile spread across her face. Boone still lay there, sound asleep. Grey almost worried that she'd get up and leave in the middle of the night. But she hadn't. She was still there in all her glorious nudity. She was long and lithe and so physically fit. Grey was a little embarrassed at her own figure next to Boone's. Grey didn't work out or anything, but she wasn't heavy. She just wasn't the fine specimen that Boone was.

Boone woke up and caught Grey watching her. She smiled.

"Hi, beautiful," Boone said.

"Hi, yourself."

"Have you been awake long? Did I miss anything?"

"I just woke up." Grey laughed. "And you haven't missed anything yet. Though I was contemplating getting up to make breakfast."

"How about you come here first?" Boone pulled Grey to her and kissed her neck. "I want some more of what I had last night."

She played with Grey's nipples, and Grey felt the contact in her nerve center. Her clit jumped every time Boone twisted or tugged on her nipples. She felt the moisture building between her legs and knew Boone would have no problem coaxing her to more orgasms that morning.

She closed her eyes and relaxed in the sensations Boone was creating. She opened her eyes when she felt Boone's kisses on her belly and knew what was next. She was so ready for Boone to taste her, to take her any way she wanted her.

Grey felt Boone's tongue lapping at her clit and clenched the sheets in her fists. She was already so close. It wouldn't take much of Boone's attentions before she came.

"Oh, God, Boone," she cried out, losing herself in the flood of her climax.

Boone held her after she came and Grey felt safe and comforted in her arms. She moved to kiss Boone's chest, but Boone stopped her.

"I'm fine for now, sweetheart. Thank you."

"Are you sure?"

"I'm positive."

"How about some breakfast?" Grey said.

"How about I just hold you for a while? Then we think about breakfast."

"That sounds wonderful."

Grey loved the feel of Boone's arm around her and the feel of their bodies meshed together. She felt like she was finally right where she belonged. And it wasn't lost on her that Boone had called her "sweetheart." She wondered if Boone even knew she'd said it.

"So what's a typical Saturday look like for you?" Grey asked.

"Depends on the season. Usually, I'll go to the bar and get the games set up, then hang out for a while. Then go back for the Ducks game and maybe have a post party at my place. And yours? What's your day look like?"

"Well, every other Saturday I volunteer serving meals at the homeless shelter. This happens to be one of my Saturdays off. Outside of that, I just lay low, or try to."

"Sounds wonderful," Boone said.

"So do you have to go get the bar ready for the day?"

"Oh, no. My weekend manager can handle it. It just gives me something to do. Personally, I'd rather stay right here right now."

"I'd like that." Grey couldn't believe her luck. Boone must actually like her, which would make her life quite wonderful. She had to admit, she'd fallen hard for her already.

"So now you ready for some breakfast?"

"How about we shower and then head out to get some breakfast?"

"I don't mind cooking you breakfast."

"And I don't mind saving you the work by buying you breakfast. Let's hit the shower. Now, where is it?"

Grey led the way and was rewarded in the shower with Boone sudsing up the loofah and rubbing it all over her body.

She then used her hands to rub the soap in further. Soon her hands were slipping and sliding all over Grey's body and Grey was a rubbery mess trying to remain upright.

Boone slid her hand between Grey's legs and, between the soap and her juices, easily slid her fingers inside her. She entered her over and over until Grey collapsed against the shower wall, spent from her orgasms.

They finished their shower and dried and dressed.

"Do you mind if we swing by my place so I can change into some clean clothes?" Boone asked.

"Sure." Grey was excited about seeing Boone's house. She wondered how it would be decorated.

She should have known. There was sports memorabilia everywhere with pictures of Ducks football players all over the wall.

"This place is so you," Grey said.

"It really is, isn't it?"

Boone disappeared to her bedroom to change her clothes and Grey sat in her den, fantasizing about going back to the bedroom and taking Boone. Boone came back out about the time Grey had worked up the nerve to do it.

Boone was wearing cargo shorts and a Ducks hoodie.

"So, what time's kickoff?" Grey asked.

"Twelve thirty."

"I assume this is the day you want me to be there?"

"I'd like that. I mean, unless you're tired of me."

"Not a chance." Grey was actually looking forward to seeing the bar, since it was Boone's livelihood. And she'd do her best to root for the Ducks, her alma mater's archenemies. She tried to make herself stop and think about what she was doing, but she couldn't. She was very much into Boone and she wasn't sure she'd be able to turn back now.

They shared a nice brunch, and Grey found herself a

bundle of nerves as they drove to The Boonies. She worried she wouldn't fit in. She worried Boone would leave her alone to go be with her friends. She had herself worked into a frenzy by the time they arrived.

She was pleasantly surprised when Boone reached for her hand as they walked to the door.

"Is this okay?" Boone said.

"What?"

"This." Boone held up their hands.

"It's great," Grey said.

"Good. Now, relax. We'll have fun."

"I will."

"I hope so, because you're awfully tense right now."

"You can tell?" Grey was surprised Boone was that tuned in to her.

"Of course. You're all knotted up." She stopped just outside the door and pulled Grey to her, kissing her lightly. "If, at any point in time, it's too much, say the word. We can always watch the game at my place."

"Thank you, Boone. I'm sure I'll be fine."

"I hope so. Just remember, I want you to have fun."

Boone held the door but didn't let go of Grey's hand. They walked in together, and it took a moment for Grey's eyes to adjust to the darkened bar. The place was packed with people in all semblance of Duckwear.

The knots in her stomach started to unwind. She relaxed as she and Boone made their way to the bar to get drinks.

"I'm going to have a beer. What would you like?" Boone asked.

"I'll have iced tea."

"Too early for wine?"

"Just a little." Grey laughed, just a little uncertain of how she felt about Boone having a beer that early.

CHAPTER NINE

Boone felt all eyes on them as they entered The Boonies. She felt Grey's grip tighten on her hand, but finally relax slightly as they moved closer to the bar.

"Where would you like to sit?" Boone asked.

"This is your territory," Grey said. "You take me with you where you'd normally go."

Boone searched the room and saw a table of regulars.

"Let's go sit with them."

She introduced Grey to her friends, including Dani, which was awkward for her, but Dani was cool. She was happy and proud to see Grey interact with everyone as they settled in to watch the game.

Boone was pleasantly surprised at Grey's knowledge of football. She participated in the conversation and rooted as loudly as anyone, which Boone knew had to be hard for her.

"How you doin'?" Boone leaned over and whispered in her ear.

"I'm having a great time," Grey said.

"You sure?"

"Positive."

Boone smiled at Grey and felt her heart soar. She'd really found someone special. She leaned in and kissed her.

"What was that for?" Grey asked.

"Just 'cause. Was it not cool?"

"It was wonderful." Grey's eyes were bright as she looked at Boone.

"Good." Boone kissed her again, this time holding her lips longer. She could get used to this.

They watched the game, and as it entered the fourth quarter, Boone was thinking about a post party.

"Hey, babe, how would you feel if I invited a few people over to my place for a barbecue after the game?"

Grey didn't miss the pet name. She wasn't sure how she felt about it. It made her heart happy, but logically, she was still undecided. Still, she wasn't the one-night stand type, and if she was going to sleep with Boone, she had to be willing to see where it would go. "Is that what you normally do?"

"I do early in the season. It'll probably be too cold for that by next week, I'd imagine. But it's up to you."

"That sounds like fun."

"Great."

"So, everyone," she said to the table. "Post party at my place."

As the game ended with yet another Duck victory, Boone grasped Grey's hand and led her back to her truck.

"You sure you're okay with people coming over?"

"I'm fine with it. Let's keep the party going."

"You're pretty awesome."

"You're not so bad yourself."

"Are you having fun?"

"I'm having a great time. I can't remember the last time I had this much fun."

"Good. Again, if it ever gets too much, just let me know."

"And what? You'll leave the party and take me home?"

"No, I'll kick them all out."

Grey laughed, which was music to Boone's ears.

"You don't think I'll do it?" Boone asked.

"I don't think I'd ask you to do that. But I'm not worried. I think it's going to be fun."

Grey helped Boone get things set up for the party. She formed burgers from the ground beef and seasoned them while Boone lit the grill. She was looking forward to meeting Boone's friends at the party. She'd met a few at the bar, but the game distracted them from actual conversation. She wondered how many people would show up. She heard voices outside and knew it was time to join Boone.

She stepped out onto the patio and was surprised at the crowd that had gathered. There had to be over thirty people in and around the pool. She located Boone over by the grill and noticed Dani talking to her.

Boone was smiling and shaking her head. Grey wondered what they were talking about.

As she walked up, she heard Boone say, "It ain't gonna happen."

"What's not going to happen?" Grey asked.

"Oh, hi, sweetheart," Boone said. She reached out and took Grey's hand. "Are you ready to meet some more people?"

"Sure," Grey said.

"Excuse us," Boone said to Dani.

Boone walked Grey around the pool area and introduced her to doctors and lawyers, business men and women and construction workers. It was quite a melting pot.

"You have an interesting combination of friends," Grey said.

"I do. We have all sorts that come to the bar. It's nice to have a variety."

"Lots of men, but quite a few women, too. That's interesting to me."

"Well, it's a sports bar, babe."

"True. I'm actually surprised at how many women are here."

"Not all sports fans are men. Just the majority of my clientele." Boone laughed.

"And the women run the gamut. They're certainly not all lesbians."

"Nope. We serve a lot of straight women, too."

"How fun."

"Thanks. I'm glad you think so," Boone said.

The afternoon passed with much drinking and merriment. The burgers were a hit and people stayed until the sun began to fade and the chill of the evening made the pool less attractive. Grey was exhausted, yet exhilarated when the last of the guests left.

"That was amazing."

"I'm glad you enjoyed yourself." Boone pulled Grey to her and wrapped her arms around her.

Grey snaked her arms around Boone's neck.

"What happens now?" She smiled.

"Well, technically, we should clean up a little."

"I cleaned the kitchen as I went," Grey said.

"So there's not much to do, then. That's a good thing."

"Yes, it is."

"Would you like to enjoy the hot tub with me?" Boone asked.

"I didn't bring my suit."

"You won't need it."

"I do like the sound of that."

Boone led Grey to the hot tub and pulled her blouse over her head.

"You have goose bumps. Are you cold?"

"A little. The goose bumps could be from something else, too, you know."

"I like that." She rubbed her hands over Grey's arms before reaching around to unhook her bra. She slid it off and tossed it to the ground.

"You've got the nicest breasts," Boone whispered. She cupped them, running her thumbs over the taut nipples. "And they're so responsive."

"They like you."

"I'm glad." She helped Grey out of her skirt then stripped down herself. "Shall we?"

Grey stepped into the hot tub, the heat of Boone's gaze on her making her wet. She sat down and Boone sat next to her, pulling her close.

"I could get used to this," Boone said.

Grey didn't know how to respond. The logical side of her told her things were moving too fast, but the rest of her loved to hear it.

"It is nice, isn't it?"

"Very." Boone nuzzled Grey's neck and kissed her earlobe.

Grey turned her head and met Boone's lips with her own. The kiss was intense, with Boone's breath hot in her mouth. She couldn't contain herself. She climbed into Boone's lap and pressed her breasts against Boone's. The feeling was electric. She knew her center was moist and ready and she craved Boone's touch. She took one of Boone's hands and placed it between her legs, not willing to wait for Boone to get there in her own time. She was rewarded by feeling Boone's fingers probing deep inside.

"Oh my God, yes," she said. "Yes, Boone. Please."

Boone stroked all her needy places and in no time, Grey held on tight as the orgasm tore through her body.

"You're amazing," Boone said.

"That was all you."

"No. You're so much fun to love."

Grey turned to straddle Boone's legs and ran her hand between them. She ran her hand over Boone's slick clit and smiled at Boone's intake of breath. Grey moved her fingers inside Boone and delved deep over and over before pulling them out and stroking her clit again. This time it was Boone who cried out when her climax hit.

Boone struggled to catch her breath and Grey snuggled into her chest, smiling with pride. It was such an honor to make another woman feel that, and she was blissfully happy to do that for Boone.

"You ready to get some sleep?" Boone asked.

"I am."

"Let's get dry and get inside. Are you okay sleeping here or would you rather go back to your place?"

"I'm fine staying here."

Boone got them towels and they dried each other off before tucking in for sleep.

❖

Boone awoke the next morning groggy but aroused. It took her only a moment to come fully awake and realize Grey was licking her nipple.

"Good morning to me," Boone said.

Grey smiled and sucked Boone's nipple deep in her mouth.

Boone ran her hand lazily over Grey's hair, loving the soft, silky smoothness of it.

Grey released the nipple and kissed down Boone's belly. Boone spread her legs as Grey reached the place where her legs met. She felt her insides tighten as Grey worked her tongue over the length of her. She felt her dip inside and arched her hips to urge her on. She was barely hanging on and when Grey moved back to her clit, she lost it, crying out Grey's name as she came.

"Thank you for that." Boone pulled Grey close. "What a way to wake up."

"I was watching you sleep and you looked too good to just let you be. I had to have you."

"Well, I'm glad you did. I'm always here for your taking."

"That's good to know."

Boone rolled over and slid her hand between Grey's legs, intent on returning the favor. She found Grey excited, clearly having enjoyed making love to her.

"Mmm. You're so wet, baby."

"Imagine that."

She deftly stroked Grey's swollen clit until Grey was gasping for air.

"Oh yes, Boone. Oh dear God, yes."

Boone kept at it until she felt Grey tense up, then issue a guttural scream as she reached her orgasm.

Boone held her again, loving the feel of Grey's naked skin against hers. She'd meant what she'd said the night before. She could easily get used to this. She didn't understand all she was feeling, but she was determined not to fight it. She just didn't want to scare Grey off with her intensity, so she kept her thoughts to herself.

"So what should we do today?" she asked.

"I hate to do this, but I really should get home so I can get some things taken care of and get ready for the week ahead."

Boone fought to hide her disappointment. "Yeah, I guess that makes sense. Can I take you to dinner tonight?"

"I'd like that."

Boone drove Grey home and headed for the bar to check

on everything. Her stomach turned when she saw Tanner's truck in the parking lot. She parked in the back and used the rear entrance, hoping to go unnoticed by her brother. No such luck.

"Hey, sis. Can I talk to you?"

"Sure. What's up?"

"Look, I've gotta come clean with you. Phoebe and I had a fight and she left me. I'm really sorry about our argument and want to tell her. Will you please help me find her?"

Argument? Argument? Boone wanted to slap her brother senseless. How dare he refer to beating Phoebe up as an argument?

"Look, I'm really sorry you and Phoebe had words." It turned her stomach to say that, but she knew she had to play along. "But I have no idea where she is. And I wouldn't even know where to start looking for her. You know all her friends. I don't. Have you checked with them?"

"I've asked everyone. No one has seen her. I'm at a loss. I miss her and am worried about her."

"Did you try her folks? Maybe she went to stay with them for a while."

"I haven't tried them."

"Well, that's my suggestion."

"Okay. Thanks. But if you see her, send her home, okay?"

"Sure thing." She lied. There was no way she'd ever let him find her.

Seeing Tanner made her realize she'd missed seeing Phoebe the day before. She'd been too wrapped up in Grey. So she cut her time at the bar short and drove out to Serene Pathway.

She found Phoebe in her room.

"What's going on, Phoebe? How are you feeling?"

"I'm tired today."

"Yeah? Well, if you need a nap or something, kick me out."

"No. I'm glad you're here, though. I feel so alone. Grey's not here on weekends, and I didn't know if I'd see you either."

"I'm sorry I couldn't make it yesterday. But I'm here now."

"How am I ever going to make it on my own, Boone? Should I just go back to Tanner?"

"After what he did to you? No way!" Boone couldn't believe her ears.

"I'm sure he's sorry."

"Sorry doesn't cut it, Phoebs. You know you can't go back to him."

"So what do I do?"

"You stay here, get counseling, and get better."

"How long will that take?"

"As long as it takes. Listen, Phoebe, Grey and her staff are trained to help women who have been hurt. Let them work their magic on you. I'm sure you'll come out of here stronger and ready to take on the world."

"I wish I had your confidence."

"Mine hasn't just been shattered. What you went through was a blow to you mentally and emotionally, as well as physically. Put it in your past, though. Commit to yourself to get better and move on."

Tears trickled out of Phoebe's eyes and she pulled Boone to her in a hug.

"How could you possibly be related to that asshole I married?"

"I've been asking myself that since he was born," Boone said. "So what did you do yesterday?"

"I spent a lot of time reading. They have a great library here."

"Oh, good. I like to hear that you relaxed for a bit."

"I'm trying. I feel so isolated here."

"You're supposed to be. Nothing to distract you from getting better."

"I need to think of it that way."

"Yes, you do."

"Thank you for coming to visit me, Boone."

"My pleasure. I'll try to come back tomorrow, too, okay?"

"Hey, Boone, what do you think of Grey?"

"I think she's a smart, capable woman, why?"

"Do you think she's gay?"

"Why do you ask?"

"I think she'd be good for you."

Boone tried to fight the blush she felt creeping over her cheeks.

"Oh." Phoebe smiled. "It looks like you might have thought the same thing a time or two."

"On that note, it's time for me to head out. I'll see you tomorrow."

"Thanks again, Boone."

"You're welcome."

It was time for Boone to pick up Grey and she smiled widely in anticipation. She couldn't wait to see her again. She was really into her and wanted to spend as much time with her as possible.

She knocked on the door and waited impatiently for Grey to open it. When she did, Boone wasn't disappointed. She was wearing a green dress that clung to her curves, while still looking casual. Boone's hormones surged. She kissed Grey's cheek.

"You look amazing."

"Thank you. But what kind of kiss was that?" She pulled Boone close and kissed her passionately.

"That was nice," Boone said. "Kind of makes me want to skip dinner."

"Oh, there's plenty more after dinner."

Boone smiled and took Grey's hand as they walked to her truck.

"So, Grey, I had an interesting conversation with Phoebe today," Boone said when they had ordered dinner.

"Is she okay?" Grey looked worried.

"Well, she's still freaking out and scared, but I figure that's normal. It was something else she said that I wanted to talk to you about."

"Do tell."

"She thinks you and I would make a good couple."

Grey choked on her wine.

"She said that?"

"She did."

"And what did you say?"

"It's more what I did."

"And what did you do?" Grey asked.

"I blushed."

"You did?" Grey laughed. "That's too funny."

"Yeah. So, what do you say? We're out at my place of work. What about yours?"

Grey sat silently for so long, Boone began to wonder if she'd pushed too hard.

"I don't know, Boone," she finally said. "I have always strived to keep my business and personal life separate. Plus, I'm still not sure what we're doing is such a good thing."

"I understand," Boone said, though she didn't really. She was crestfallen.

"No, I'm not sure you do. Because I'm not sure I do anymore. I don't suppose it would hurt for people to know I'm seeing someone. And don't get me wrong. I'm not embarrassed or anything. I simply try to keep things separate, as I said. And I think I need to figure out what I'm doing here."

"So that was just a yes and a no at the same time," Boone said.

Grey laughed uneasily.

"I know. I'm sorry. Let's just say okay and see what happens."

"Okay? So like I can tell Phoebe about us?"

"Sure. Why not?"

Boone broke into a wide grin.

"That's great! Thank you."

"Oh, Boone. I'm sorry if I made you worried."

"I'm sorry if I made you uncomfortable. I don't want to push you too hard, but I really like you."

"I like you, too. And I don't understand it. Because you represent everything I'm against."

"But you've been to the bar. It's not a bad place. And I'm not an abusive alcoholic. I'm not going to hurt you."

"I'm still leery, Boone."

"Well, if you're not in this for the long haul, what the hell are we doing? Just sleeping together? Because it feels like more."

"It feels like more to me, too, Boone. Honest. I'm sorry. I just get so confused when I try to sort things out in my mind."

"Good. So, we'll agree that it's more than just sex and you'll quit overthinking it." Boone smiled.

"I promise I'll try."

When they arrived back to Grey's place, she turned in the truck to look at Boone.

"Did you want to stay the night?"

"I'd like that very much."

"So would I."

They made their way to Grey's bedroom, where Boone slowly and deliberately undressed her.

"Did I tell you how much I love this dress?" She dropped it to the floor. "It really showed off your figure."

"I'm glad you like my figure."

Boone moved her hands all over Grey's body.

"I love your figure."

Grey took her bra off and stepped out of her panties, leaving herself bare for Boone, who quickly undressed and pulled Grey onto the bed. She covered her with kisses while she skimmed her hands all over her, finally stopping when she arrived at her center.

"I love your body," she said.

"And I love yours." Grey ran her hands over Boone's back, down to her firm ass and back to her shoulders. "And I love how you love mine."

"Mmm-hmm." Boone was lost in the feeling of Grey's heat. She continued to please her and was rewarded with Grey crying out in ecstasy.

Grey quickly returned the favor, plunging her fingers deep inside Boone. Boone writhed on the bed under her, needing more as she grew close to her climax. She held her breath as her body tensed and released as her orgasm hit.

Chapter Ten

Grey relaxed into her routine with Boone. She spent her days hard at work and her nights enjoying their time together. She really liked Boone and surprised herself how quickly she'd let herself fall into the relationship. They fit so well together and were very compatible. She still couldn't believe she'd almost written Boone off for owning a sports bar. Her patrons all seemed nice enough. Of course, she of all people knew you couldn't tell. After all, Phoebe's husband frequented The Boonies.

She was able to focus on work, although she was happy things had slowed down for a while. She was working hard on her current clients. Phoebe was making progress and working twice a week with Connie to try to bolster her job skills. Grey sat with her one day in her office.

"You're doing so much better, Phoebe. I'm proud of you."

"I feel a little better."

"Good."

"I look in the mirror and there are only a few cuts and bruises left to remind me what a mess I was."

"You need to remember you didn't do that to yourself."

"I hear you and Boone say that. But I still think part of it had to be my fault. Why else would he have done this to me?"

"Because he's sick. He's a sick man with a need to hurt people."

"But he'd never beat me like this before."

"But he had hurt you."

"Sure, he grabbed my arm too hard. Or twisted it or pulled my hair."

"And you think that's normal?"

"You and Boone don't go through that, do you?"

"Of course not."

"But you're still new and exciting. Tanner was sweet to me in the beginning, too. Before we were married. I keep wondering if we can go back to that."

"Do you really believe you can?"

Phoebe sat quietly and Grey would have loved to have been inside her head right then. She'd love to know the process she was going through.

"I don't know. I sure want to believe that."

"But can you? Can you honestly put yourself in the position to risk another beating like that again?"

"No. I don't want to. You're right, Grey. I can't do it, can I?"

"That's got to come from you, Phoebe. You need to believe and accept that."

"But you'll help me be strong, right? You and Boone?"

"We'll always be here for you. Now, let's talk about how your meetings with Connie have been going."

The rest of the session went well, and Grey walked back to her office to work on her notes. She was typing away when Boone came in.

"Hey there," Boone said, fighting the urge to kiss Grey.

"Hi, yourself. How's your day been?"

"Good. And yours?"

"Not bad."

"Have you seen Phoebe today?" Boone asked.

"You know I can't discuss my residents with you."

"I didn't mean like in a session. I just wondered if you'd seen her."

"I'm sure she'll be happy you're here."

"Nice avoidance." Boone laughed. "I'll head back to find her right now."

"I think you'll find her in the kitchen," Grey said.

Boone walked toward that end of the facility and found Phoebe working away with two other women, presumably preparing dinner.

"Hey, Phoebs."

"Hi, Boone."

"Do you have a couple of minutes?"

"Sure."

"You look great. Are you feeling good today?"

"I am. I had a really good session with Grey today."

"Good. I'm glad to hear that."

"And I'm really looking forward to my session with Connie tomorrow. I want to find a job and start moving on with my life."

Boone pulled Phoebe to her in a tight hug.

"That's fantastic. Really, really good news."

"I couldn't have done this without you, Boone."

"I don't know about that. But if it's true, I'm happy I could help."

"You have come to see me almost every day. And you've shown me that people do care about me. I don't have to settle for someone who doesn't."

"That's right. And don't you ever forget that."

"I'll try. I'm glad you came out here and all, but I need to get back to work helping make dinner."

"Sure thing. Enjoy and I'll see you tomorrow."

She walked back to Grey's office, but she was gone. She was disappointed she didn't get to see her again. She wanted to talk to her about plans for the night. She knew they'd be together, but didn't know where they'd be. She figured they'd figure it out later.

She drove to the bar for happy hour. The place was jumping and she helped out behind the bar for a while before her phone rang. Grey's name appeared on the screen, and she stepped outside to take the call.

"Hey, babe."

"Hi, Boone. I'm sorry I missed you leaving."

"Me, too. But I figured you got busy."

"I had sessions."

"That's cool."

"So, dinner tonight? Where and when?"

"What are you in the mood for?"

"Besides you?" Grey said.

"I like the way you think."

"I feel like Italian. How does that sound?"

"That sounds great. I make a mean chicken parmigiana."

"Okay, so dinner at your place. I'll be there around six."

"I'll see you then."

Boone went back in to help out for a little while longer, then headed to the grocery store to shop for what she needed for dinner. She was busy in the kitchen when the doorbell rang. She smiled to herself as she answered it and found Grey standing there with her overnight bag.

"You know, babe," Boone said, "I was thinking. You really don't need to ring the bell when you get here. You can just walk in. Especially if I'm expecting you."

"Really? You're ready to take it to that level, huh?" Grey smiled.

"I think I am."

"Sounds good to me. Now, kiss me, please."

Boone was happy to oblige. She kissed Grey softly on her lips, savoring the feel of them.

"That was nice," Grey said. "By the way, the house smells amazing. You really do know how to cook, don't you?"

"I hope it'll taste as good as it smells. I'm just finishing up the salad now. Come on into the kitchen with me."

She handed Grey a glass of wine and resumed making the salad. She served them up and they sat at the table that she had set, complete with taper candles she'd bought.

"Are you trying to romance me, Boone Fairway?"

"Guilty."

"You're doing a fine job."

"Thank you."

"I love how romantic you are," Grey said.

"I love everything about you," Boone said.

Grey paused, her fork halfway to her mouth. She stared blankly at Boone.

"I'm sorry. Too much?"

Grey walked to Boone. She bent over and kissed her hard on her mouth.

"Not too much, Boone. Not too much at all."

"Good. Because it's true. I'm crazy about you, Grey."

"I'm crazy about you, too, Boone. Now let's eat before the food gets cold."

After the dinner dishes were cleaned, Boone took Grey's hand and led her back to her bedroom. She felt the connection between them like never before, and she wanted to savor the night. She sat on the bed and pulled Grey to her lap. She kissed her tenderly, lovingly.

She cupped the back of Grey's head and pulled her in for another kiss. This one was more intense than the first, with her tongue probing Grey's lips for entry to her mouth. Grey's lips parted and when Boone felt their tongues meet, the familiar pulsing began between her legs.

They fell back onto the bed and Boone caressed Grey's cheek.

"You're so beautiful," Boone whispered. "I can't get enough of you."

She fondled Grey's breast through her blouse, reveling in the responsive nipples that poked her. She slipped her hand under the blouse and pushed Grey's bra out of the way so she could tease the nipple with her fingers. She tugged and twisted it and smiled as Grey arched into her touch.

Grey finally pushed Boone off her and stood.

"I need to be naked with you. Now." She quickly undressed and lay back in bed, watching Boone strip out of her own clothes. Boone joined her and hugged her to her body, enjoying the skin-on-skin contact. She kissed her again, unable to get enough of her sweetness. She kissed down her chest to her pert nipples and licked one and then the other. She sucked one into her mouth while her fingers played with the other. Grey's nipples grew longer at her coaxing and she continued until she could stand it no longer.

She reached her hand between Grey's legs and felt the welcome liquid there.

"I love how you're always ready for me."

"I always am."

Boone dipped her fingers inside and coated them with Grey's essence. She dragged her fingers to her hard clit and rubbed circles around it, teasing her.

"Please, Boone. Please rub me. I need you."

Boone felt that she had dragged it on long enough and pressed her clit just like she knew Grey liked it. Grey grabbed Boone's head and pulled her in for a frantic kiss just as the orgasm ripped through her.

Grey rolled over on top of Boone and continued kissing her. Boone ran her hands the length of Grey's body, pressing her closer.

Grey kissed down Boone's body until she climbed between her legs. She kissed and nipped at her inner thighs. Boone lay there, enjoying the sensations, but waiting impatiently for what she knew was next. She finally felt Grey's hot breath on her center and tensed even more.

She felt Grey's tongue inside her and knew she wouldn't last long. Making love to Grey always aroused her to the breaking point. When Grey moved her tongue to her clit, she held her in place and moved in the same rhythm as her tongue. She felt the ball of energy burst inside her as she reached her climax.

Boone pulled Grey to her and held her close as they drifted off to sleep.

❖

Boone and Grey were at The Boonies watching a Ducks game one chilly Saturday afternoon when Tanner walked in.

"Oh shit," Boone said.

"What's up?" Grey asked.

"That's Tanner." Boone pointed him out.

He looked around the bar until his gaze finally landed on them. He started in their direction.

"Oh shit, he's coming over here."

"It's okay. I promise not to castrate him publicly," Grey said.

"Hey, sis. How you doin'?"

"Good, Tanner. No work for you today?"

"I work too fucking hard already. They wanted us to work today, but I told 'em where they could put that."

"I'm glad you're feeling flush," Boone said.

"I'm not. They pay us like shit, you know?"

Boone's stomach was in knots. She was horribly embarrassed that Grey knew this lowlife was her brother.

"I need a drink." He turned and walked to the bar.

"He's a real charmer," Grey said.

"Isn't he? I'm sorry, Grey. If I had my way, you wouldn't meet any of my family."

"He seems like he's already been drinking."

"That's just his personality."

"If you say so."

The game started and Boone turned her attention to it. By halftime, the Ducks were ahead by thirty points. She was happy, but when she looked at Grey, her spirits fell.

"What's wrong?" Boone asked.

"Your brother."

"What about him?"

"He's been drinking a lot, Boone."

"Babe, please. Don't worry about him. We both know he's got a temper, but I won't let him hurt you."

"I'm just saying they should cut him off. Look at him. He can barely stand up."

"I'm telling you, he's fine. Please, relax and quit thinking about him."

"And, Boone, I'm telling you I can't relax. If you let your bartenders serve people until they're snockered, that's a real problem."

"They don't."

"They do. Tanner's living proof. Who knows better than I what people are capable of when they get three sheets to the wind?"

"Are we back to blaming sports bars for domestic violence?"

"I just think your bartenders are being irresponsible and that's a direct reflection on you."

"Are we having our first fight?" Boone asked.

"It may be our first and last. I don't know if I can keep seeing you."

"What? Look, I'll just continue to counsel my bartenders on overserving. It's the law and we follow it. You need to trust me. Remember trust? You have my word."

"If you promise. But, Boone, I'm serious about this."

"So am I."

"Then go tell them not to serve Tanner anymore."

Boone stood and took a deep breath. Tanner was such an asshole. She wasn't looking forward to the confrontation. But if it would make Grey happy, she had to do it. The thought of losing her scared her more than her brother did.

"Hey, Tanner," Boone said. "You need to take it someplace else."

"What the fuck? You're tossing me?"

"Not exactly. You're welcome to stay here, but you're cut off from booze."

"So I'll switch to beer."

"No, you're cut off for today, Tanner. You're messed up."

"I'm fine. And when did you get so holier than thou?"

"I care about my business and I'm not going to let you get plastered here. You're cut off for today. Go home and sleep it off. You want me to call you a cab?"

"I'm not even drunk, Boone. I'm not going home. I'll go to another bar that'll take my money. Fuck you."

She watched him walk out and then called her bartenders and waitstaff into a huddle.

"Be careful, okay? I know everyone's having fun, but please watch out for people drinking too much. We need to cut people off before they get blitzed. Got it?"

She worked her way back to Grey, somewhat miffed at her for making her do that. Deep down, she knew Grey was right, though. She sat next to her and took her hand.

"Thank you, Boone," Grey said.

"You're welcome. I know you were right, anyway."

"I need to know you're being responsible with your patrons. Your job is critical in that area."

"I know. I can't have people driving away under the influence and I certainly can't have people driving home to beat up their significant other."

"I hope you're not patronizing me."

"Not at all. I'm serious."

"Good."

After the game, they went out to dinner.

"Were you serious about leaving me?" Boone asked.

"I don't know. I think I'd have to if I didn't feel you were being responsible at the bar. Irresponsible bartenders and owners are a threat to society."

"I've never thought of myself as irresponsible."

"Just please keep on your employees not to be, either, okay?"

"Okay."

They ate in silence for a few minutes.

"I'd be crushed if you left me," Boone said.

"It wouldn't be easy for me, either. But I have to do what's best for what I believe in. And that's a huge issue for me. Drunk people."

"I thought alcohol didn't necessarily lead to abuse."

"While studies show that, you and I both know it lowers inhibitions. So someone who normally wouldn't hurt another person might do it when they're drunk."

"That makes sense."

"Either way, please make sure your staff aren't afraid to cut people off. Even the Tanners of the world."

When they got back to Boone's place, she pulled Grey to her and held her.

"I don't like fighting with you."

"It's not fun," Grey said.

"I'm glad we're okay now."

"We are."

Boone kissed Grey passionately, hoping to erase any doubt she had. Grey returned the kiss and Boone felt the heat rise inside her.

She walked Grey down the hall and they stripped each other's clothes off before climbing into bed together. Boone kissed Grey again and ran her hands over her breasts, alternately kneading the firm mounds and squeezing the hard nipples. Boone grew wetter as she moved her mouth to Grey's breasts and sucked and licked them. She finally dragged her hand down Grey's body and ran it between her legs. She loved her as she'd learned to, paying special attention to her slick clit. Grey came in no time, squeezing her legs around Boone's hand.

Boone lay back and Grey returned the favor, kissing and sucking Boone's nipples and breasts, her hand between her legs. She rubbed Boone's clit before sliding inside her.

"More, baby. Please, more."

Grey continued to move in and out until Boone felt herself clamping on Grey's fingers as she came.

Chapter Eleven

Grey went about her business at work and continued to enjoy her time with Boone. But the issue of the sports bar constantly weighed on her mind. She tried to let it go, but couldn't. Boone had held a staff meeting and urged them to get better about not letting people drink too much, but even Boone had to admit it was easier said than done. But Boone was also determined to lead by example, which Grey felt was critical. And Boone had offered to be the one to cut someone off if she was there.

So Grey told herself to relax and go with it. She was just crazy about Boone, and outside of the bar issue, life was great. Although the bar was a pretty huge part of their relationship.

She continued her work with Phoebe, who was making great strides. Connie had even lined up some job interviews for her. Everything was going well. She had a few new clients, and Boone still came out every day to visit Phoebe. Grey loved that Boone was such a caring person. She truly cared about Phoebe and she truly cared about Grey. Grey did not doubt that at all.

She was working in her office when Boone walked in, looking harried.

"What's up, babe?" Grey asked.

"Nothing. Just a rough lunch rush at the bar."

"Want to talk about it?"

"I had to kick Tanner out again."

"I'm sorry. But good for you for doing that."

"I always worry that he'll just find another bar, though."

"And you figure you're losing money then?" Grey said.

"What? No. That's not it at all."

"I hope not."

"How could you even think that?"

"I don't know. I just wonder."

"No, I worry he's just going to keep getting drunker elsewhere and getting more and more dangerous."

"I hope that's not the case."

"So do I." Boone paused for a moment. "How's Phoebe today?"

"She's great. I don't know where you'll find her right now."

"Is she in a session?"

"No. I'd start in the common room."

Grey watched Boone walk off and felt a weird sensation. Something wasn't right. She couldn't put her finger on it, but something just didn't feel right.

When Boone stopped by her office on her way out, Grey mentioned it.

"Boone, is everything okay?"

"Things are fine. I just had a rough day is all."

"And you blame me, don't you?"

"How could I blame you?"

"I just feel like you do."

"That's just crazy. I don't blame you."

"I've complicated your business by being in your life."

"Grey, you've done no such thing. We're simply being more responsible now. There's nothing wrong with that."

Boone kissed her.

"I'll see you tonight."

Boone drove back to the bar, Grey's words heavy on her mind. Did she blame Grey for being more responsible? Did she resent the implication that she wasn't doing enough before? That was ridiculous. If Boone could help keep one woman from being abused, it was for the good. She felt good about laying down the law at The Boonies. After all, it was legally required. She knew it put her bartenders and wait staff in touchy situations, but for the most part, they were few and far between. Most of her clientele knew their limitations and didn't push them.

She wondered if Grey was having second thoughts. She sure hoped not. But she knew the bar had been a major contention when they first met and could see it getting that way again. She determined to relax and make the evening special.

After the bar, Boone stopped by the florist and bought an autumn arrangement to use as the centerpiece. She picked up a couple of steaks and a nice bottle of wine. She really wanted to have a romantic dinner with her woman.

Grey arrived and Boone greeted her with a warm hug and a kiss.

"Hi, baby," Boone said.

"Hi, Boone. Do I smell baked potatoes?"

"You do. And now that you're here, I'll fire up the grill."

"Oh, you're in your element tonight, aren't you?"

"I am." Boone laughed.

She took Grey's hand and walked her to the kitchen where she poured her a glass of wine.

"You relax," Boone said. "And I'll go get the grill going."

"I'll join you," Grey said. "Is there anything I can do to help?"

"Nope. This dinner's on me. You just enjoy yourself."

Boone put the steaks on the grill and turned to Grey. "I really like you, you know that, right?"

"Of course I know that. And I really like you, too."

"I love hearing that." She kissed Grey's lips, as always awed by their softness.

They took the steaks off and sat down to dinner.

Boone was still uptight, feeling something wasn't right, but she told herself to relax and enjoy her dinner. Her insecurities won out.

"So, we're good, right?"

Grey set down her utensils and looked at Boone. Boone felt the knot in her stomach grow.

"I hope so, Boone."

"You hope so?"

"I don't know. I know we're good together, but I don't know."

"What don't you know?"

"I have concerns about the bar."

"Babe, you've been to the bar how many times now? You know it's not some horrible place that's a constant drunkfest. It's a gathering spot where people socialize, watch games, and hang out. You know it's not the center of evil."

"I know all those things. But I still know how many people are abused after sporting events. And by intoxicated people. Your bar is against everything I spend my life working for."

"So what do you want from me?"

"I don't know, Boone. I don't know."

"You keep saying that. You're making me nervous."

"Maybe we need a break."

"A break?"

"I need some time to think, Boone."

"Fine. You can think and still be with me. I'd be fine with that."

"You know what I mean. I need some space to decide if this is what I really want."

"People would give anything to have what we have," Boone said. "Please don't walk away from this."

"You know my childhood, Boone. But you don't know I was in a relationship with an abusive alcoholic for seven years. I have issues with this and I'm not sure I can overcome them."

Boone was stunned. The thought that anyone could have hurt Grey made her furious, and the thought that the pain inflicted by that person might interfere with what they shared only made it worse.

"I get it, Grey. I do. But again I say, you've been to The Boonies. You've seen that our patrons are good people. I still don't think you should call it quits on us because of the bar. And as far as abusive alcoholics, you've seen me have a few beers. I'd never be abusive."

"I'm sorry."

"Is that all you can say? But what about my feelings for you? Do they not count for anything?"

"They do, Boone. They means the world to me, and I'm sorry to have to do this. I do care about you, but I can't compromise myself to be with you anymore."

"Grey, please. I'm begging you."

"I'm sorry, Boone. But I'm afraid I have to."

Boone sat still and watched Grey walk out of her house and out of her life.

❖

Boone tried to wrap her head around a life without Grey. She went to the bar the next morning and worked, but she felt numb as she went through the motions. There was a large void inside her. A void she doubted would ever be filled again.

She helped her staff during lunch, and when it was over, she sat down and had a beer. She knew she needed to go see Phoebe, but wasn't sure she could stand seeing Grey, knowing she couldn't kiss or hold her. But she couldn't turn her back on Phoebe.

She drove out to Serene Pathway and walked into the office. Grey looked so beautiful sitting at her desk, she almost turned and left. How was it possible that this woman no longer shared her life?

"Hi, Grey," she said quietly.

"Hi, Boone."

"Is Phoebe around?"

"She actually is at a job interview."

"Really? She didn't mention that yesterday."

"It was kind of last minute. The company called Connie today and asked if we had anyone, so we sent Phoebe."

"Do you think she's ready?" Boone asked.

"I wouldn't have let her go if I didn't think so."

"I guess that's true."

Boone stood uncomfortably. She knew she had to leave, but she wanted to reach out to Grey and ask her to please rethink her decision. Boone knew in her heart of hearts that they belonged together and felt that deep down, Grey knew it, too.

"Okay, well then, I guess I'll take off. Let her know I stopped by, please."

"I will."

"I'll see you later."

She drove back to the bar and grabbed a beer. She sat at the bar watching baseball. She didn't care who was playing or who was winning. She only cared that Grey had left her. She had another beer and then another. She lost track of time when Dani sidled up next to her at the bar.

"What are you doing here so late?" Dani asked.

Boone looked up and noticed it was after six.

"I guess I lost track of time."

"Well, you'd better get home and get dinner ready for the little woman."

"I should get home." Boone stood and wobbled a little on her feet.

"You okay?" Dani said.

"I'm a little tipsy," Boone admitted.

"You need a ride home?"

"If you don't mind."

"I don't. So, everything okay with you?"

"Not so much, but I don't want to talk about it."

"Okay," Dani said. "Let's get you home."

They arrived at Boone's house and Dani walked in with Boone.

"You want me to help you with anything?" Dani said.

"No, I'm fine. Thanks for the ride."

"So, is there trouble in paradise?"

"I told you I don't want to talk about it."

"I can help you forget." Dani moved close to Boone. She wrapped her arms around Boone's neck.

Boone peeled Dani's arms off her.

"Not a good idea. Thanks, but no thanks."

"Okay, but if you change your mind, you know where to find me."

Boone felt alone after Dani left and wondered if she should have taken her up on her offer. But she knew she'd made the right decision. Dani wasn't Grey. No one was or ever would be.

❖

Grey threw herself into her work. She doubled her sessions and worked on her outreach program. Every day felt emptier than the day before, no matter how hard she worked. She worked all day and went home every night to an empty house. She hadn't anticipated just how hard life would be without Boone. They had gotten so close so fast and it had felt so right. She just wished Boone didn't own a bar where people like Tanner hung out. Boone was right. Most people at the bar were responsible in their behavior. But not all. And it reminded her too much of everything she fought so hard against in her life. But she missed Boone terribly.

She set up speaking arrangements at local schools. She was visiting a local university and there was a large turnout. She was starting to feel better about things. She had several people come up to her after her presentation to sign up as volunteers. Things were definitely looking up. She glanced up from her signup sheet to see a tall, attractive woman with short gray hair and steel blue eyes looking at her. Her heart stopped as she looked into the eyes. They reminded her so of Boone's.

The woman smiled a soft, knowing smile.

"I admire your work," she said.

"Thank you."

"I'm Professor Carnes, but you can call me Sarah."

"It's nice to meet you," Grey said.

"I'd like to buy you coffee and talk to you more about your shelter."

"That would be great. Let me get my things put away here."

"Can I help?"

"No, thanks. I've got it." She packed her bag with the signup sheet and her pamphlets then turned to Sarah. "I'm ready now."

Sarah walked her to the student union and the coffee shop inside. She ordered their drinks while Grey found a table in the corner. Something about Sarah made her feel very comfortable, which made her very uncomfortable and nervous.

Sarah joined her and set the coffees down.

"They're cinnamon express. I hope you like it. It's my favorite."

"Sounds good to me," Grey said.

"I should start by telling you I'm a professor of women's studies."

"That's good to know. It also explains your interest in my shelter."

"All women should be interested in your shelter."

"I agree."

"So, I'd like to set up a program with you and my students."

"How so?" Grey asked.

"I'd like to make it part of my curriculum for them to volunteer a couple of hours a week at your place."

"Well, while I appreciate the offer, I don't know if we could accommodate that many volunteers."

"Fair enough. What would be more realistic?"

"Maybe four hours a term?"

"That's all?" Sarah sounded surprised.

"Well, how many students are in your classes?"

Sarah laughed.

"I have over two hundred students a term. I suppose I wasn't thinking very clearly, was I?"

"That's okay. I appreciate your enthusiastic offer. I just want to make sure we can accommodate all the help. And I think an additional four hundred hours a week would be extreme."

"Okay, well what about offering students to volunteer

there as one of the projects in the class? I often give them choices of real life opportunities every term for a major portion of their grade. Can I list your shelter as an option?"

"That would be great," Grey said.

"Excellent. We should meet again to hammer out the details."

"Sounds good." Grey took the last sip of her coffee.

"How about over dinner next week?"

Grey was immediately uneasy. She felt like she was being asked on a date and didn't know how to answer.

"I'm sorry," Sarah said. "You look like you've seen a ghost. Is dinner too much?"

"No, I'm sorry. It was just so unexpected."

"Was it? You're an attractive woman. We had a nice time over coffee. We clearly have much to talk about. Why is dinner such a stretch? Oh, wait a minute, are you involved with someone?"

Grey sat silently. No, she wasn't involved with anyone. Much as she'd like to be, she'd ended things with Boone and had to accept that. But was she ready to date again so soon? She chided herself for being so foolish. Why not go out with Sarah?

"I'm not involved. I was until recently, though. I guess I'm just a little gun shy."

"Understandable. I'm sorry if it was a bad experience," Sarah said.

"It wasn't a bad experience." Grey struggled to explain. It had been wonderful. Boone was an incredible woman and had been a fantastic partner. What could she say to Sarah? "We split up amicably. She and I just weren't on the same page."

"How so?"

"It's complicated." Grey knew it sounded lame.

"It always is," Sarah said. "So no to dinner?"

"Dinner would be fine," Grey said before she could stop herself. She felt bad hurting Sarah over feelings for Boone that she knew she needed to get over.

"Somehow I feel like you're settling for it, rather than excited about it, but I'll take it. I'd enjoy more time with you and I look forward to getting to know you better."

Grey knew Sarah was trying to be nice, but her words just made Grey more uncomfortable.

"So, do you want me to pick you up for dinner or how would you like that to work?" Sarah went on as if Grey was completely agreeable.

"Why don't we meet somewhere?" Grey suggested.

"Sure. How about La Hacienda? They have great margaritas there."

"That sounds great. Wednesday at seven work for you?"

"That will be perfect," Sarah said. "I look forward to it."

She walked Grey out to her car.

"I really enjoyed meeting you," Sarah said.

"It was nice meeting you, too."

"I look forward to Wednesday," she said as Grey climbed into her car.

"Me, too," Grey lied. Nothing could be further from the truth.

CHAPTER TWELVE

Boone was spending way too much time at the bar. She knew this but couldn't help it. She had no desire to do anything else with her time. She'd even given up on her visits with Phoebe. Phoebe got the job, so was working all day and then helping at the shelter, where she still lived, at night. Boone had seen her a couple of times, but Phoebe was really too busy in her new life to worry about. Besides, the only time she could really visit her was in the evening, and by then Boone had normally had too much to drink.

Dani was a constant at Boone's side, offering her comfort in her time of need. Boone kept saying no, though she missed the company of a woman. She missed Grey more, and that was what kept her from enjoying Dani or anyone else.

Work was busy and she used that as an excuse to spend all her time there. It was too cold for pool parties at her house by then, but she still had people over after the games on Saturdays to maintain some sense of normalcy in her life. But after the people left, she was alone again, and the void that filled her threatened to consume her.

She was tempted to call Grey every day, but knew the sound of her voice would be too painful and recognized it wouldn't do any good. She only wished she knew what she could do to convince her to come back to her, short of selling the bar. She'd actually entertained that thought on occasion, but it was her life and losing it would be almost as painful as losing Grey. And she couldn't take that kind of pain again.

Boone was enjoying a beer after the lunch rush one day when Tanner came in, already weaving as he walked.

"Tanner, you know we can't serve you if you're drunk," Boone said.

"Fuck you. I don't need to drink at your dive. There are plenty of places where I'm welcome."

"Then why are you here?"

"I wanted to tell you. Someone saw Phoebe the other day. Apparently, she's working for some accountant. I've got his card at home. I'm gonna go by there and tell her it's time for her to get her crazy ass home. No wife of mine is going to be working."

"It's been a long time, Tanner. Maybe you should just let her go."

"Bullshit. She's mine. She's coming home with me."

"Where's your pride, bro? She left you. Let her go."

"Whose side are you on? That bitch is gonna learn not to leave me again!"

"Oh, aren't you a big man, picking on a woman."

"What? What do you know? She needs to learn her lesson."

"For what? For leaving a drunken bastard of a husband?"

"Watch your language, or I'll give you some of the same."

"Oh, I'm scared," Boone said. "You sound so tough, threatening your big sister."

"You should be scared. You're too big for your britches sometimes. Someone needs to take you down a notch."

"Tanner, get out of here. Get out of my bar now!"

"I'm leaving. I've got more important things to worry about than you anyway."

Boone watched him leave. She gave him five minutes before she jumped in her truck and drove to Serene Pathway.

"Is Grey here?" she asked Cecelia as she burst through the office door.

"She's with someone right now."

"How much longer? I need to talk to her. It's critical."

"She should be out in about ten minutes. Have a seat. Is there anything I can help you with?"

"It's about Phoebe. She's in danger."

"Okay. Let's wait for Grey, then."

Grey walked in ten minutes later and paused in the door when she saw Boone, who immediately stood.

"I'm sorry to barge in on you like this," Boone said, her heart racing at the sight of Grey. "But it's important."

"What's going on?" Grey asked calmly.

"Tanner came by the bar. One of his friends saw Phoebe at work. Tanner plans to go by the accountant's office. What do we do?"

"Well, we filed a restraining order against him before she started the job, so if he shows up, he'll be arrested."

"He didn't mention any restraining order to me."

"Of course not," Grey said.

"Are we sure it was served?"

"Yes, it was."

"Okay, then…" She ran a hand through her hair. "He plans to take her back and teach her a lesson for leaving him. I'm scared for her."

"I'll call the accountant's office and alert them."

"Can I pick up Phoebe from there now? Can I bring her here?"

"Sure." Grey handed Boone the accountant's card with his address on it. "Do you know where this is?"

"I can find it. I'll get her and be back here."

Boone hurried out of the office and plugged the address into her phone. She sped off down the road, following the voice giving her directions. She arrived at the accountant's office and asked for Phoebe.

"Are you from Grey's place?" the woman at the front desk asked.

"I am."

"We were expecting you. Let me go get her."

Phoebe came out, eyes wide with fear. She latched on to Boone.

"Thank you for coming."

"Of course, Phoebe. I want to keep you safe. Let's get out of here now."

They drove back to Serene Pathway, with Boone keeping an eye on her rearview mirror the whole time, terrified Tanner would somehow follow them. They arrived back at the shelter without incident.

Phoebe moved into Grey's embrace.

"Why does he have to be that way?" Phoebe cried. "I want to be safe. I want to move on. I don't want to live my life in fear anymore."

"I'm sorry, Phoebs," Boone said. "But I couldn't take a chance the way he was talking."

"I appreciate it. I guess I'm lucky he's such a loudmouth sometimes, huh?"

"Well, there is that."

"What about my car?" Phoebe asked. "It's still there."

"We'll go get it," Grey said.

Boone was startled by Grey's statement. The idea of riding

back with Grey both thrilled her and terrified her. It would be sheer torture to have her that close for that long.

"Sure we will. You want to go now before he gets there and sees it?" Boone asked.

"Yes. We should."

Boone and Grey walked to the truck in an uncomfortable silence.

"Thank you for coming to tell us," Grey said when they were in the truck.

"Of course. He was threatening me today, too. I wasn't taking any chances."

Grey turned in her seat to face Boone.

"He threatened you?"

"Yep. Said I needed to be taken down a peg or two, or words to that effect."

"Do you think you're safe? Are you worried? He knows where you live."

"I'm not worried. He wouldn't hurt me. Or he'd die trying, I'll tell you that."

Grey laughed. The soft sound melted Boone.

"You don't think I mean it?" She sounded gruffer than she'd intended.

"I'm sure you do," Grey said. "I'm sure you do."

They arrived at the accounting office, and Boone was both happy and sad as Grey stepped out of the truck. She paused with the door open.

"Are you going back to the shelter?" Grey asked.

"I am."

"Okay. I'll see you there."

Boone found Phoebe in her room, curled into a ball on her bed. She sat next to her and placed her hand on her shoulder.

"It's going to be okay, Phoebe."

"You don't know that." Phoebe's voice was muffled by her pillow.

"I do. Neither Grey nor I would ever let anything happen to you."

Phoebe rolled over, her face splotchy from crying.

"But don't you see? I can't stay here forever. I need to be able to live my own life. And it felt so good to have a job and to feel like freedom was in my future. Now I'm back to square one."

"No. No, you're not. When you came here you were scared of your own shadow. You've grown leaps and bounds. And you've tasted freedom. And we'll make sure you get it always. And soon."

"Yes, we will," Grey said from the door. She walked in and sat in a chair next to them. "This is a temporary setback. And it's only a precaution."

"How can he still ruin my life? I've moved on. Why can't he?"

"He's a sick man," Grey said.

"I should have had him arrested in the beginning," Phoebe said. "But he would have just come out angrier than he already is. I was hoping he'd have a new girlfriend by now and have forgotten about me."

"He's not that type," Grey said. "He's going to hold on to the hope of getting you back. We've talked about this."

"But I still hoped."

"That's only natural," Boone said, unsure of her place in the conversation, but not wanting Phoebe to feel wrong to want to believe the best.

"Hope is what keeps us all going," Grey said.

Boone wanted to ask if she could ever hope for Grey to come to her senses and come back to her, but knew it wasn't the time or place. Still, the way Grey looked at her, she couldn't help but wonder if she still cared. If her hope was going to ever pay off.

Feeling uncomfortable, she stood.

"I should probably get going."

"No!" Phoebe grabbed her hand and pulled her back down. "Stay."

"Yes, Boone. You're welcome to stay. There's no reason to run off. Why not have dinner here tonight?"

"Will you be staying?" Boone asked.

"Would you rather I didn't?"

"No, I'd be happy if you did."

"Then I will. It'll be a nice treat for me."

Boone wasn't sure if she was referring to the fact that Boone would be there or just having dinner with her residents, but she didn't care. She was just happy to have more time with Grey.

"If you'll excuse me, I've got some work to wrap up," Grey said.

Grey felt lighthearted as she left the room. She still had strong feelings for Boone. She didn't know how wise it was to agree to dinner. She'd said okay without really considering things. Being with Boone would be wonderful, but also torturous. She reminded herself that it was her idea to end things with Boone and she had to live with that decision.

She was in her office when a reminder popped up on her phone. Dinner with Sarah. She had completely forgotten about planning on meeting her for dinner. While she wanted to work with her about internships, she would rather keep things professional, and meeting her for dinner wasn't professional. And now she had a valid reason to cancel. She dialed the number on the card Sarah had given her.

"Hello?" The soft voice on the other end almost made Grey feel guilty. Almost.

"Hi, is this Sarah?"

"It is."

"Hi, Sarah. This is Grey Dawson. From Serene Pathway?"

"Oh, yes. Hello, Grey. What can I do for you?"

"I hate to do this, but we've had a crisis here and I'm not going to be able to make dinner tonight."

"I'm sorry to hear that. I hope everything is okay?"

"It will be. I just need to be here right now."

"I understand. Can I get a rain check?"

"Sure. I'll call you and we'll set something up."

Grey hung up, feeling relieved. She truly wasn't ready to date and didn't know why she'd agreed to it in the first place.

She went to work charting her notes on the residents she'd counseled that day. She pulled up Phoebe's chart and entered in the events of the day. She reread what she'd written and felt her anger at Tanner coming back. She needed to step back and remain professional. Would she feel this intensity if it was someone besides Boone's sister-in-law? She vowed to help Phoebe get back on her feet as soon as possible. The sooner she was out, the sooner Boone would be out of her life. Maybe then, Grey would be able to forget about her and move on.

For the moment, though, Grey was almost giddy at the idea of spending the evening with Boone. She finished her work and went to the kitchen to let them know she and Boone would be there for dinner. She ignored the questioning looks from some of the women and made her way back to Phoebe's room. Her heart skipped a beat at how handsome Boone looked, sitting there talking to Phoebe. She had to clear her throat to speak.

"You two ready for some dinner?"

Boone stood and Grey fought to keep from moving into her arms. She didn't know what was wrong with her. She was beginning to doubt if ending things had been the right thing to do.

"I'm not really hungry," Phoebe said.

"It will be good for you to eat something," Boone said.

"She's right," Grey said. "Come with us. You just need to eat a little."

Phoebe joined them and they walked to the dining room. Dinner was a chicken casserole with a salad and rolls. Phoebe served herself little portions of everything while Boone served up a healthy plateful.

Grey missed cooking for someone who appreciated food as much as Boone did. She told herself to snap out of it as she served her own plate.

The feeling around the table was tense, the conversation sparse.

"So, why don't you all tell us about your day?" Grey said.

A few women spoke up, but most stayed quiet. Grey didn't know if it was her presence or Boone's or just the activities of the day, but clearly the women were uncomfortable. She wondered if she could slyly let Boone know they should leave.

She needn't have worried. Boone quickly finished her dinner and stood.

"I hate to eat and run, but I need to get home. Thank you all for your hospitality." She hugged Phoebe. "I'll see you tomorrow."

"I'll be here."

"I'll walk you out," Grey said.

They got to Boone's truck, and Grey was at a loss for words.

"I'll see you tomorrow, huh?" Boone said.

"Sure thing. Thanks for everything today, Boone."

"No problem. I wasn't going to let anything happen to Phoebe."

"Well, I appreciate it."

"What's going to happen now?" Boone asked.

"What do you mean?" Grey's imagination ran wild.

"I mean how long does Phoebe have to be off work? Can she go back there? Or will she need to find another job? And how do we keep this from happening in the future?"

Grey fought not to let her disappointment show. Of course Boone was talking about Phoebe.

"She'll just take a few days off. Hopefully, Tanner will show up and they can tell him she doesn't work there. That's all we can hope for. If you see him, you can ask him so we'll have some idea of where he is in his plans."

"I will. I'll find out if he's been there or not."

"Thanks, Boone."

They stood there awkwardly, Grey searching for something else to say and Boone not saying anything.

"Well, I guess I should get going," Boone finally said.

"Yeah. I'll probably be heading home soon, too."

"Thanks again for dinner," Boone said. "Though I don't think the others appreciated my presence much."

"That was a little uncomfortable, wasn't it?"

"I just think they like their routines and didn't appreciate an interloper."

"It could have been me, too. I can't tell you the last time I had dinner here."

"Or it could have been us."

"I suppose there is that," Grey said.

"Oh, well. Whatever it was, it won't happen again. I won't stay for dinner again."

"I think it helped Phoebe, though."

"I hope so. But she'll be better tomorrow. And the day after. She'll be independent again soon."

"Yes, she will."

"Okay, well, I guess I'm going to head out. I'll see you tomorrow."

Grey watched Boone climb into her truck and stood in the driveway long after her truck was out of view.

CHAPTER THIRTEEN

Boone was anxious all morning the next day. On one hand, she really wanted to see Tanner. On the other, he was the last person she wanted to see. She made it through the lunch rush and grabbed a beer. She sat at the bar and pondered what to expect at Serene Pathway that afternoon. She had really enjoyed her time with Grey the day before. She felt like Grey had enjoyed it, too. Especially at the end. Maybe it was her imagination, but she really didn't think Grey had wanted to say good-bye. She wondered if she should ask Grey to get back together, but told herself no, that was up to Grey. And Boone couldn't take the rejection if Grey said no.

She was about to leave when she saw Tanner's truck pull up. She calmed her stomach and willed herself to act nice.

Tanner walked in and sat next to her.

"What's up, sis?"

"Not much. How you doin' today?"

"I'm doin' good. How come you're so nice today?"

"I'm always nice," Boone said.

"You were a raging bitch last time I was here."

"You pissed me off."

"Whatever. Can I buy you a beer?" Tanner said.

"Sure, why not?"

The bartender brought them each a beer. Boone sipped hers and fought not to sound too interested when she finally got the nerve to broach the subject.

"So, did you find Phoebe?" she asked.

"No. Turns out she doesn't work there. My friend was wrong."

"That seems like a cruel thing to do. Tell you he saw her when he wasn't sure." She wanted to fish for as much information as she could without being too obvious.

"Well, he's an idiot. I don't know why I believed him."

"So, you ready to let her go now? Admit she's gone and not coming back?"

"Hell, no. She's still my wife. I'll find her. And I still think you know something."

"What could I know?"

"You tell me. I mean, I saw her car here then it was gone and you say you didn't see her. I don't believe you. I'll never believe you."

"Well, I don't know what to say. We've gone over this a million times. I didn't see her and I have no idea where she is. I just think it would be healthier for you if you moved on."

"You and all your healthy bullshit. You wouldn't let some bitch just walk out of your life, would you?"

"First of all, I wouldn't be with someone I considered a bitch." Boone felt her anger beginning to flare again.

"You would if she just left you."

"I'd hope not."

"You're so fucking pious."

"And you wonder why I get mad at you."

"You think you're so much better than I am. And you're not. We're both from the same parents. I'm not some scummy low-class citizen while you hang with the upper middle class. We're the same. You just think too highly of yourself."

“Tanner, why do you bother? Why do you come here? If you hate me so much, why do you come to my bar? Why do you buy me beers? It doesn’t make any sense.”

“I just like to remind you where you come from. And I know eventually you’ll slip up and tell me where Phoebe is.”

“Even if I knew, I’m not sure I’d tell you.”

“You bitches stick together. But you do know. And I’ll find out from you. And then you’ll feel like shit and it’ll all be worth it.”

“I need to get going. It’s been a real pleasure,” Boone said.

She drove out to Serene Pathway, her mood foul. Even the promise of seeing Grey couldn’t elevate her spirits. Tanner was wrong. They were nothing alike. Sure, they had the same parents, but she grew out of that. He was the spitting image of their father. And he was proud of it. It made her sick.

She parked her truck and got out. She was surprised to hear a car pull up next to her. She turned to see Tanner’s truck. She felt a cold fist grip her stomach. She walked over to him as he got out.

“How did you get in here?”

“I drove in right behind you. They didn’t have time to close the gate.” He laughed.

“What are you doing here?” she asked.

“I could ask you the same thing.”

“A friend of mine lives here.”

“I bet. What’s her name? Phoebe?”

“What? No. What are you doing here?” she repeated.

“I just wanted to see where you were going. So, take me in to meet your friend.”

“Why?”

“Because I care about your friends.”

“Bullshit.”

"Are you going to take me in or am I going to go in by myself?"

"You're not going in. Get in your truck and get out of here."

"No chance, sis. You seem too anxious for me to leave. Now I really need to know who's in there."

He walked to the door.

"Tanner!" Boone called. "Get the fuck out of here!"

He turned and smiled at her. "No way."

The door opened and Grey stepped out.

"What's going on out here? What's with all the yelling?"

"Grey, you remember my brother, Tanner. Tanner, this is Grey. She's the friend I was telling you who lives here."

"Hi, Grey, it's nice to meet you. Won't you invite me in?" Tanner said.

"Why are you here?"

"I like to know friends of my sister."

"Bullshit. You followed me out here because you have some inane idea that I know where your ex-wife is. I keep telling you I don't. Now you've met Grey, who lives here, so you can leave," Boone said.

"She's my *wife*, not ex." He turned back to Grey. "This is a big house for just one person to live in. You don't have any roommates?"

Boone looked at Grey, her stomach still tight. She knew Grey wouldn't blow it, but she also knew Tanner wasn't taking no for an answer. And the minute he stepped in the house, he'd see it was much more than just a house. They had to keep him out.

"I don't have any roommates. And I'm not accustomed to strangers showing up and demanding entrance to my house. I'll thank you to leave now."

"I'm not a stranger. I'm Boone's brother. We're practically family."

"I'm afraid I don't see it that way," Grey said. "Will you leave or should I call the cops and have you arrested for trespassing?"

"What a fucking bitch! I'll leave. But I'll be back. I think you have something to hide. And I'm going to find out what."

Boone stood by Grey and watched Tanner pull out of the driveway.

"I'm so sorry," Boone said.

"How did that happen? How could you not have noticed him following you?" Grey was clearly pissed.

"I was lost in my thoughts. I'm sorry. I really never dreamed he'd follow me out here."

"Now our whole operation is compromised. I don't know what I'm going to do."

"I'm so sorry, Grey." Boone was at a loss. She didn't know what she could possibly say to make things right. "I guess I should leave."

"No." Grey sighed. "He's gone. The damage is done. Let's just get inside."

"What do I tell Phoebe?" Boone asked.

"That's a really good question."

"On one hand, I think she deserves to know," Boone said. "On the other, I don't want her to be afraid. She's safe here, right?"

"I hope so, Boone. I really hope so. I hope Tanner bought that I'm just a friend and I live alone."

"I can't believe he followed me here."

"I can't believe it, either."

Boone was filled with emotions. She was embarrassed to have let Tanner follow her, she was ashamed that she'd disappointed Grey, and she was still filled with hope to rekindle things with Grey. Although that last one probably wasn't going to happen, thanks to Tanner.

Grey and Boone stood in the kitchen sipping coffee.

"So, back to Phoebe," Grey said.

"Yeah. What do I do?"

"I think we need to be honest with her. We need to tell her exactly what happened."

"What about his threat that he'll be back?"

"I don't think we need to mention that bit," Grey said. "Let's go see where she is, so you can see her."

They walked back to the office and Grey scanned Phoebe's schedule.

"She's meeting with Connie right now," she said. "She should be out soon."

"Why is she meeting with Connie? She already has a job, right? She can go back there now that Tanner thinks she doesn't work there, can't she?"

"Boone, you know I can't discuss her sessions with you."

"Yeah, but…"

"No buts. I can't. She can, if she chooses, but I will not."

"That's fair. I'm sorry I asked. I guess I just forget that I'm not part of her treatment plan." She laughed weakly.

Grey smiled. She felt bad for Boone. She knew Boone felt horrible and only wanted to help. But she'd allowed Tanner to follow her. Grey knew she should be angrier, but she couldn't stay mad. It wasn't like Boone had invited Tanner there.

"I think you are part of her recovery, though," Grey said. "I think your visits here do wonders for her. It's always nice to know that not everyone on the outside has forgotten about you."

"That makes me feel a little better."

Grey reached out and took Boone's hand. She squeezed it lightly before releasing it.

"You're a good person, Boone Fairway." She witnessed emotions flash across Boone's face before she regained her composure. Grey cleared her throat. "Phoebe should be out of her session now. Why don't we go to her room?"

Grey followed Boone down the hall, admiring the tall, trim form in front of her. She was having serious second thoughts about their breakup. She tried to remember her logic of calling it off, but it seemed to make less and less sense as time went on.

"Hey, Phoebs," Boone said.

"Hi, Boone." Phoebe's face lit up. "I'm so glad you're here. I've had a great day and want to tell you about it."

"I'm glad you've had such a good day, Phoebe," Grey said. "I'd like to hear about it, too."

"Sure. So, Connie said I can go back to work Monday. They're fine with me coming back. And they're all understanding of my situation. Isn't that great?"

"That's wonderful," Boone said.

"Yep, and I guess Tanner actually went by there, but they told him I didn't work there. I doubt he'll go back, right?"

Boone looked at Grey, who was having second thoughts about the whole honesty approach.

"I don't know Tanner that well. Boone, what do you think?"

"I doubt he'll go back there. I think if they told him you didn't work there, he'll believe it. He may want you back, but I don't think he's smart enough to think someone would lie to him."

Phoebe was focused on Grey. She seemed not to have heard Boone.

"What did you mean, Grey?"

"About what?"

"You said you don't know Tanner that well. How do you know him at all?"

"Can we sit down?" Grey asked.

"You're making me nervous."

"Phoebe, Tanner followed me out here today," Boone said.

"What? He *what*?"

"I'm sorry, Phoebe. I'm so sorry."

"Where is he?" She jumped up and pulled her curtains back, looking out at the yard.

"He didn't stay. He didn't even get inside," Boone said. "Grey heard us yelling outside and came out. She made him leave."

"How'd you do that? Does he know I'm here?"

"No," Grey said. "I told him I lived here and if he didn't leave I'd call the cops."

Phoebe sank down on her bed.

"He'll be back. Did he believe you? Why would he? He'll be back. I can't stay here now."

Boone sat and put her arm around her.

"There's no reason for him not to have believed Grey."

"But he found out where I worked. And now where I live. He won't stop until he finds me."

"Don't forget you have a restraining order against him. He can't get to you. We can call the cops any time," Grey said.

"But will they get here in time?"

"We won't have to worry about that. He won't be back," Boone said. "He has no reason to come back."

Grey stared at Boone. They both knew he'd threatened to come back. She wanted to call Boone out on it, but opted instead to follow her lead.

"She's right. He has no reason to think this is anything but my home."

"I hope you're right," Phoebe said.

"You're safe here," Grey said.

"So tell us more about your day," Boone said.

"I was feeling really good about work. I felt like soon I'd be able to get my own place. I know Grey has a list of housing places I could afford soon. But now I'm scared again. I have Grey here to protect me now, but at my own place, I won't have anyone. I'm not so excited anymore. I'm just scared again. And I'm tired of being scared. And I'm pissed. Excuse my language, but I am. That bastard needs to move on and forget about me and leave me alone."

"I'm trying to get him to do that," Boone said. "Every time I talk to him, I try to convince him it's time to move on. I'm hoping eventually he'll listen to me."

"Thank you, Boone. For everything." She leaned into Boone's shoulder and the tears flowed freely.

Grey felt like she was imposing. Her gaze locked with Boone's and her stomach fluttered. She turned and left, walking to her office to work on her paperwork.

She couldn't focus on her work, though. Her thoughts kept turning to Boone. She knew she should be angry with her for letting Tanner follow her. She knew Boone owned a bar and she was against that as a concept. However, she felt hypocritical since she'd had nothing but good times when she'd gone to The Boonies with Boone. She sighed and placed her head in her hands. She was so conflicted.

"Penny for your thoughts?"

Grey looked up to see Boone leaning against the door frame. "Nothing worth a penny."

Boone shoved off from the door frame and walked behind Grey. She placed her hands on her shoulders and began to rub.

A moan escaped Grey before she could stop it.

"I'd say you needed this, huh?" Boone said.

"I guess I did," Grey confessed as she leaned back into Boone's strong hands.

"So, why the exasperation? Are you stressing over Tanner?"

"Not really. Although I suppose I should be."

"I don't know. Sometimes he just blows hot air."

"But we both know what happens when he acts."

"Yes, we do."

They were silent and Grey realized her reaction to Boone's touch was more than enjoying a massage. She placed her hand on Boone's.

"Thank you for that."

"My pleasure. Hey, Grey, I'm really sorry about today. I feel horrible about Tanner."

"It wasn't your fault, Boone."

"It was totally my fault."

"You didn't do it on purpose is what I meant."

"No. I would never put this place or you or Phoebe in danger."

"And I appreciate that."

"So, um, look. I'd like to make it up to you. Can I buy you dinner?"

"Do you think that's a good idea, Boone?"

"I think it's a great idea or I wouldn't have suggested it." She smiled and Grey melted.

Grey was torn. Dinner with Boone sounded wonderful. Too good. But they weren't an item and it wouldn't be right to go out with her, would it? Would she be giving Boone false hope? Or was she giving herself false hope?

"I suppose one date wouldn't hurt." The words were out before she realized what she'd said.

"Date? I was just thinking dinner, but if you want it to be a date, that's fine by me."

Grey felt the blush creep over her face.

"I'm sorry. I meant dinner. One dinner won't hurt."

Boone just smiled. Grey felt stupid, but she couldn't take back what she'd said. Boone was right. It was just dinner.

"I'll meet you at six?" Boone said.

"Where?"

"La Trattoria."

"Oh, good. Italian sounds good. I'll see you there."

Grey wrapped up her day in the office. She went to check on Phoebe and found her in the dining room having dinner. She seemed relaxed, so Grey just let herself out of the shelter and headed to meet Boone.

Grey was nervous when Boone walked in. She felt like a schoolgirl on her first date. She told herself she was being ridiculous, but she couldn't calm herself. When Boone walked in, she feared she'd swoon.

"Hi, there. You ready for dinner?" Boone seemed so relaxed. Grey took a deep breath to steady herself. "You okay?"

"I'm fine. Let's eat."

The conversation was easy, and Grey found herself less at ease than she had been. Boone was such a fun person. She couldn't relax, though. She kept questioning whether it was wise to be out with her. It didn't help her resolve to not get back together with her.

"You sure don't seem like you're having fun," Boone said.

"I'm sorry." She didn't offer an excuse. She was searching her mind for one when her cell phone rang. She checked it. "It's the shelter."

"Take it."

"Hello? This is Grey."

"Grey! We need you. There's a man here yelling at

security. I can see him through the cameras. The guard says he keeps demanding to see you. He's loud and belligerent. I'm scared."

"I'm on my way. Call the police. They'll get there before I do."

"What's going on?" Boone asked as Grey stood.

"I have to go."

"What's happening?"

"My guess is that Tanner's back."

"I'm coming with you."

They climbed into Grey's car and sped off.

They arrived in time to see Tanner being placed in a police car. Grey approached an officer who was talking to her night manager.

"I'm Grey Dawson," she said. "I own this place."

"This guy says he's trying to find someone named Phoebe. You know anything about that?"

"I can't talk about any of my residents. But I can tell you he was here earlier looking for her, too. I told him then that I live here. That this is my residence. It's critical that he not know otherwise."

"Got it. We haven't said anything to him. And we won't. We'll take him in for trespassing and public intoxication. We'll have his truck towed, too. He won't be bothering you again tonight anyway."

"Thank you, sir."

The officer walked off and it was then that Grey realized Boone was standing next to her. She leaned into her strong arms and let herself be comforted. It only lasted a minute.

"We need to go check on Phoebe."

CHAPTER FOURTEEN

They found Phoebe huddled in the corner of her room. She was rocking back and forth, crying uncontrollably.

"I heard Cecilia on the phone. Tanner was back, wasn't he?" she said.

Boone went to her and pulled her into her arms.

Phoebe allowed her to hold her briefly before quickly becoming enraged. She pummeled Boone's chest.

"This is all your fault!"

Grey didn't know what to do. Before she could cross the room, Boone had taken Phoebe by her wrists and held her arms down.

"I don't blame you for being mad at me," she said. "But violence isn't the answer. You know that."

"But he wouldn't have come here if not for you. Now what do I do?"

"He still thinks this is my house," Grey said. "You're safe here."

"That's what you told me earlier. And look what happened."

"He's gone now," Grey said. "The police took him away. He won't be back."

"The police took him? You had him arrested? Oh, God. He's really gonna be pissed. Can't you do anything right?"

"He was arrested for trespassing and public drunkenness," Boone said. "He saw Grey talking to the cops as he was being loaded into the car. He thinks this was all her doing. You need to trust us, Phoebe. Now more than ever."

"Why?"

"Because if you don't, and go off all half-cocked, you'll be in a lot more danger than you are here. Grey's not going to let anything happen to you. And neither am I."

"Please continue to trust us. We'll continue to keep you safe."

Phoebe was silent. She seemed to have calmed. Boone had her cradled against her chest.

"I hope you're right," Phoebe finally said. "I really hope you're right. I don't feel very safe right now."

"That makes sense," Grey said. "You're scared. And Tanner's a scary man. But we won't let him near you. It's important that you get past your fear. You need to move on with your life. You're making a better life for yourself. You've come so far. You can't backslide now."

"I understand what you're saying. But you make it seem so easy. You don't know Tanner."

"I know men like him. I've known plenty like him in my life, Phoebe. And I know you will win this battle. Because you deserve a life of happiness."

"I do?"

"Yes, you do," Boone said. "And you'll have it. You just have to believe in us. And in yourself."

"I wish I had as much faith in me as you guys do."

"You've learned to over the time you've been here," Grey said. "You just need to remember all you've learned and not let it all slip away."

"I'll try."

"Good. Are you going to be able to get some sleep? Or do

you want to go watch some TV? What would you like to do?" Grey asked.

"I think I'd like to be alone. I'll just read until bedtime."

"Okay," Grey said. "If you need one of us, you just call, okay?"

"I think I'll be okay. I feel better now. Thank you."

Boone walked Grey back to her office and waited while she charted notes about what had happened.

"I really admire you and the work you do," Boone said.

"It's not easy, but the success stories outweigh the failures, which makes it all worthwhile. And I really believe Phoebe will be a success story."

"I sure hope so."

"May I ask why you're still here? You don't need to stay, you know. I think she's fine."

"Actually, I was hoping you'd give me a ride back to the restaurant to pick up my truck."

"Oh my God," Grey said. "I completely forgot about that. I'm sorry. Let's go."

"Only if you're ready."

"There's nothing left for me to do here tonight. Tanner's not coming back. Phoebe's under control, and my staff knows how to reach me if they need me."

"Great then. I'll take that ride now."

They drove to the restaurant in silence. Boone wanted to talk to Grey about her feelings, but felt it was an inappropriate time. She wanted Grey with every fiber of her being and didn't know how much longer she'd be able to be around her without acting on it.

Grey parked next to the truck and turned to face Boone.

"Thank you for all you've done," she said.

"I haven't done much good. I let Tanner find the shelter. I'm responsible for this whole mess."

"But you were there for Phoebe after. And it's not really your fault. How could you have known he'd follow you? Much less come back? And you helped keep me calm during the whole ordeal. For this I'm grateful."

Boone watched Grey's lips move. They called to her. She quit thinking, quit doubting herself, and leaned in for a kiss. Their lips met and the familiar fire surged inside her. When she felt Grey respond, she grew dizzy with need. She put her hand behind Grey's head and pulled her closer.

When the kiss ended, Boone looked into Grey's eyes.

"Should I apologize?"

"I don't think so."

"But you're not sure?"

"I'm so confused, Boone."

"I'm sorry. I'll get going."

She felt Grey's hand on her arm.

"Please don't go. Not yet."

Boone leaned back in her seat.

"I don't know what to say, Grey. I still have feelings for you."

"And I have feelings for you."

"So why are we fighting this?"

"I wish I could remember."

"It's all because of the bar. And that's not going anywhere."

"I know. But it all made sense at the time. And now it's all jumbled in my mind."

"Maybe I need to give you more time to sort through your feelings," Boone said.

"It's just that you and your staff are irresponsible and I can't respect you for that. I need to know that you won't overserve people to the point of intoxication."

"You don't respect me?" Boone couldn't believe her ears.

There was no reason for that. "I work hard at what I do and I do the best damned job I know how to do. You have a misguided notion of what running a bar is."

"I know it requires the guts to cut people off sometimes and I don't see you or your staff having those guts."

"I've told you. We've had meetings. We've stepped up awareness. I don't know what else you want me to do."

"I want it to stop," Grey said. "I want it no longer to be an issue at The Boonies."

"You're being unfair," Boone said. She was making leaps and strides to try to make sure her bar was following every letter of the law. She resented being told she wasn't.

"I'm being honest, Boone. And you need to be honest with yourself. You have the party boi image and you like it. But part of that means getting drunk at the bar and letting others do the same. It's not okay."

"But you had fun with me. At the bar. You can't deny that."

"I would just like to see you enjoy it with less alcohol being served."

"I don't think we have an overserving problem. Maybe we did, but we've gotten better. I think you're the one with problems. And you need to get over them and learn to trust. I'll see you around."

Boone climbed out of the car and slammed the door. She was pissed and wanted Grey to know it. She drove home to her empty house and poured herself a drink. She took one sip and thought of Grey's words.

To hell with her, she thought as she tossed back the rest of her bourbon.

❖

Grey was miserable the next day at work. She tried to focus on anything she could put her mind to, but nothing was working. She was afraid she'd finally ruined her chances with Boone for good. But that was a good thing, right? The bar was an issue for her. So why was she so upset and on the verge of tears all day?

She saw her residents and did her counseling, making sure to be present for each one. But as soon as a session would end, she'd think back to the hard look in Boone's eyes the night before. She didn't like being called out on her faults, that was for sure.

But neither did Grey. And she had to ask herself if she was the one who needed help. If her issues with alcohol and trust were things she needed to work on. No, she told herself. She was a healthy woman. Boone and her staff overserved and that was just the way it was.

She was sitting at her desk when she heard the familiar voice, now cold and distant.

"Is Phoebe here?"

Grey turned to see Boone looking as handsome as ever in a black Ducks hoodie and faded blue jeans. Her stomach flopped. Life would be so much easier if she didn't want Boone as much as she did.

"Boone," she said. "About last night…"

"You said your piece. We don't need to rehash it. Now, about Phoebe?"

"She's here somewhere. I don't know where, though."

"I'll find her."

Grey watched Boone walk down the hall and wiped away one of the tears that had been threatening all day. Damn it. Why did this have to be so hard? Up until last night, she'd known Boone would take her back if she just said the word.

Now that would never happen. She needed to accept it and move on.

She went back to charting her notes and left early, not having it in her to face Boone again. The next day was more of the same. She tried to make sure she was in with a resident when she thought Boone would arrive, but Boone surprised her by showing up earlier than she'd expected.

"Why are you here so early?" Grey asked.

"Not much for me to be doing at the bar once the lunch rush is over. Before, I'd stick around and have a couple of beers, but I'd hate for someone to overserve me, so I left."

Grey felt her stomach clench.

"I don't appreciate the sarcasm."

"Whatever. Can we talk about something else?"

"Sure. Phoebe had a good day. She's chomping at the bit to get back to work."

"I bet. I'm going to go see her right now."

"Okay."

"Are you going to sneak out of here again? Or will I get to say good-bye?"

"I'm sorry about yesterday. You were just so mad. I had to leave."

"I was mad. I was pissed. Partly because of what you said to me, but partly because you may have been right. I don't like thinking we're overserving people at the bar. I don't like the idea that we might serve the beer that pushed someone over the edge and lends them to violence. I've fought my whole life not to be like the people I was raised with. I don't want to have anything in common with my dad or my brother. So you struck a nerve with me in a big way."

"I'm sorry. I should have been more delicate in my delivery."

"It's hard to be delicate about saying someone's irresponsible."

"Boone, that's not what I said."

"It's what I heard, though."

"So, let's go out tonight to celebrate your new devotion to moderation," Grey said.

"What? You want to go to dinner to show me how smug you are at being right?"

"That's not what I'm doing, Boone. You're not being fair."

"Oh, and you are?"

"You can be so frustrating!"

"Right back at you."

"I simply thought that it might be nice to go have dinner. That's all. No more, no less."

"And you think that continuously asking me out while making sure we're not together anymore isn't frustrating? Seriously?"

"I'm sorry. I guess I didn't think of it that way," Grey said quietly.

"Yeah, well, maybe you should. One of us never wanted that relationship to end, okay? And it wasn't you. And it's not easy to be asked out but not be allowed to be involved with you."

"This isn't the time or the place to discuss this."

"There isn't any discussion. Or is there?"

"Let's go to dinner tonight, Boone. Please?"

"Fine. I'll meet you at La Hacienda at six. And now, if you'll excuse me, I'm off to find Phoebe."

She found Phoebe in the common room, watching television.

"How you doing, Phoebs?"

"I'm okay. I miss my job. I can't wait to get back there."

"We just need to make sure the coast is clear."

"I know. I hate that he has so much control over me still, Boone."

"He doesn't, Phoebe. It was a last-ditch effort coming here. He won't be bothering you anymore."

"I hope you're right."

"I am."

"Thanks for coming to see me, Boone, but I need to get into the kitchen to start dinner prep. I'll see you tomorrow?"

"Count on it."

Boone walked out through the office. Grey was still sitting at her desk.

"That didn't take long," she said.

"No. She's busy."

"Well, thank you for coming out to see her, Boone."

"She's an important part of my life. Of course I'm still going to visit her. Regardless of you and me."

"And you show her that. I appreciate that."

"Okay, well, I'm out of here. I'll see you tonight."

CHAPTER FIFTEEN

Grey left work early, too edgy to focus any longer. She felt horrible for upsetting Boone as she had. Clearly, she still had feelings for Boone. Was she right to continue to deny them? The bar wasn't going to go away. This much was true. But bars existed all over the place. It wasn't fair to judge Boone by her way of life. And she worked hard at her job. She was a respectable business owner, just like herself. She shouldn't judge her. She was all jumbled in her thoughts. Her heart was begging her to get back together with Boone, even though her mind continued to have doubts.

And Boone had said she and her staff were working on overserving their clients, so Grey really didn't have that as an excuse anymore. She was so confused. She drove home and looked longingly out at her garden, being pelted by the Portland downpour. She wished she could sit out there and meditate on everything to come to some sort of resolution.

She picked up a book, hoping to distract her mind, but that didn't work, either. She poured herself a glass of wine to try to relax. She wondered if Boone would need a beer to relax before their date.

Not a date. Dinner, she reminded herself. There was no way Boone would have a date with Grey after all she'd done.

So, maybe all this thinking and wondering was moot. It really wouldn't matter how Grey felt if Boone didn't want to get back together. Not that that's what Grey wanted. Or was it?

❖

Boone watched the rain fall on her pool, wishing she could get in and swim some laps to relieve her tension. She was still pissed at Grey and confused at why she insisted they go out again. What could it possibly accomplish? Grey would simply repeat all the reasons she had for not dating Boone, and Boone would be left feeling like a second-class citizen. She'd worked so hard to overcome that, and she didn't like to be called it, especially not by someone she loved. Yes, she still loved Grey. She couldn't deny that. And sometimes she felt like there was a chance Grey loved her, too. But then Grey had said some pretty mean things to her, which made her doubt that love.

It was finally five o'clock so Boone hopped in the shower, letting the hot water wash away some of the frustration she was feeling. All she could do was hope for a nice evening that didn't end in name-calling or accusations. She would be fine if it ended that way.

She dressed and headed for the restaurant. She saw Grey's car there already and felt a rock in the pit of her stomach. Not knowing what to expect made her anxious and dreadful. Still, it was time with Grey, which she craved.

Boone climbed out of her truck and took a deep breath. She walked into the restaurant and saw Grey sitting there in a navy skirt and a boat neck blouse. She looked beautiful.

"You look very nice," she said.

"So do you," Grey said. "And you smell good, too."

"Thanks."

Boone stood there looking down at Grey, unsure of what to say next. Grey stood.

"Shall we get a table?"

"Sure."

They were shown to a table and again, Boone was at a loss for words. Grey didn't seem to have anything to say either. The awkward silence grated on Boone.

"So," Boone said. "How was the rest of your day?"

"It was fine."

"Good." She couldn't believe how strained things were between them. Clearly, this had been a bad idea.

"Look," she said. "I don't know if this is such a good idea. I could leave now and you can enjoy your dinner in peace."

"No. I wanted to have dinner with you. If I'd wanted to have dinner by myself I would have."

"It just doesn't seem like either of us has much to say."

"Actually, I think we both have a lot to say, but we're unsure where to start."

"I don't know about that. I pretty much said all I had to say at the shelter today."

"I don't think you did. I think we both have a lot more on our minds that we need to talk about."

"Look, the bottom line is that you think I'm a lowlife scum who owns a business that encourages people to beat up on each other."

"That's so not true, Boone. Nothing could be further from the truth."

"Oh, no?"

"Okay, I have reservations about the bar. But I feel that way about all bars, not just yours. And maybe it's not fair to feel that way."

"Maybe?"

"I'm trying here, Boone. It's hard. I'm having to shift my whole way of thinking. I'm having to consider things differently than I have my whole life."

"No one's making you. And you're not having to anymore anyway, since you cut me out of your life."

"Don't you get it? I'm trying to say I'm confused."

"What about?"

The waiter came by and took their order. Boone was irritated at the interruption, but ordered her dinner and handed over her menu.

"Anyway," she said. "You were saying something about being confused?"

"It's not easy to simply turn my feelings off."

"You seem to have done a good job of it so far."

"But I told you what concerns I had and you've addressed them."

"So what? You know I still care about you. That doesn't change your perception of me and my livelihood."

"You make it sound like I have a horrible perception of you," Grey said.

"You do. You think I'm an irresponsible bar owner who encourages domestic abuse in her patrons."

"I don't. I just know that potential is in you. And yes, I think you tend to serve too much, which could lead to an abusive situation."

"But I've told you I've instructed my staff not to overserve. I believe they'll be more aware of it."

"Yes. For a whole day or two."

"Hey," Boone said. "It's a start."

"It is. I'm not knocking it. It's a very good start. But you can see why I'm still hesitant."

"What do you mean?"

"I'm still confused about whether I want to get back with

you after only a day or so. How do I know you won't start overserving again?"

Boone's heart skipped a beat. Had she heard correctly?

"Wait, there's a chance you'd take me back?"

"Well, of course. That's what this is all about."

"Why didn't you say so? I thought you just wanted to have dinner to ream me again."

"No, Boone. I've been miserable without you. Surely you know that."

"How could I possibly have known that?"

"Did you miss the kiss the other night?"

"Well, no."

"Okay then. I've been so confused these last few days. Wanting you, but knowing I had issues with the bar. It's been so hard."

Dinner was served then, with Boone again irritated at the poor timing.

"But now that the overserving is under control, you'll take me back?"

"Promise me you'll stay aware of it."

"I promise." Boone smiled. She was the happiest woman in the world at that moment.

"Okay. We can try again. And trust me. I know the bar issue is something I need to work through. It's my issue and I'll do my best to get past it."

"I appreciate that."

"It's the least I can do."

They ate their dinner with pleasant conversation, talking about Phoebe and life in general. Boone was feeling more relaxed than she had in days. When dinner was over, they walked out to the parking lot. Boone walked Grey to her car. She pressed her against it and kissed her hard. Grey responded, wrapping her arms around Boone's neck and pulling her close.

When the kiss ended, Boone waited until she found her breath.

"So, when can I see you again? I mean, I'll see you at the shelter, but can we go out again tomorrow night?"

"Why wait?"

"What do you mean?"

"Boone?"

"Yes?"

"Go get in your truck. I'll follow you home."

Boone's heart soared. She kissed Grey again quickly, then climbed into her truck. She couldn't wait to get home.

She was a bundle of nerves as she parked her truck and watched Grey pull in behind her. She was excited and happy to have her back where she belonged, but she felt bad that Grey was still somewhat conflicted. Still, she told herself, Grey was a grown woman and could make her own decisions. And Boone was thrilled she'd made this one.

She walked over to the car and opened the door.

"How you doin'?" she asked.

"I'm okay," Grey said.

"You know, we don't have to do anything," Boone said. "I can just hold you if that's what you need."

"I think what I need is you in all ways."

"Are you sure?"

"I'm positive."

Boone extended her hand and helped Grey out of the car. She pulled her into her arms and kissed her hard. Grey kissed her back, her hands running through Boone's hair.

"Let's get inside," Grey said.

Boone led her inside and they walked to the bedroom.

"I'm nervous," Boone said.

"You? You've done this a million times." Grey laughed.

"I just want it to be right."

"It will be, Boone. With you it's always right."

Boone kissed Grey again, allowing her tongue to meander slowly and tenderly into Grey's mouth. The kiss was soft and heady, and Boone knew she was right where she belonged.

She unbuttoned Grey's blouse and felt the gooseflesh beneath it.

"You're so beautiful," she said, sliding the blouse to the floor. "I love you."

She realized what she'd said and bent to kiss Grey again before she could object.

"Oh, Boone," Grey said after the kiss. "I love you, too. I always have."

Boone kissed her passionately as she deftly unhooked her bra and tossed it to the floor. She laid Grey on the bed and lay next to her, running her hand over her breasts. She paused to pinch a nipple and was rewarded when Grey let out a long moan.

Grey arched into her touch and Boone bent to kiss her other breast. She kissed all over it before dragging her tongue lovingly over the pert nipple. She finally drew the nipple deep into her mouth and felt Grey's fingernails digging into her back.

"Oh, God, Boone."

Grey pulled away and stood and hurried to strip out of her skirt and underwear. She stood bare before Boone, who couldn't look away from the sight before her.

"Come here, baby," Boone said.

"Not until we get you out of those clothes," Grey said.

Boone stood and quickly undressed, then lay back on the bed.

"Come here."

Grey climbed on the bed and straddled Boone's stomach, rubbing into her as she played with her own breasts.

"Oh dear God, are you trying to kill me?" Boone asked, mesmerized by the sight.

"You like this?" Grey asked.

"Very much."

Boone slid her hand between them and felt Grey's swollen clit. She took it between two fingers and rubbed until Grey pinched both her nipples and cried out, collapsing on top of Boone.

"Oh wow, that was amazing," she said.

"You're amazing," Boone said, rolling over to suckle Grey anew. She slid her hand down Grey's belly, into the wetness she'd helped create. She slipped her fingers deep inside and felt the warmth close around them. She moved them in and out as she ran her tongue over Grey's nipple.

"Oh God, Boone. Oh dear God, that's it. That's the spot."

Boone kept her fingers in deep and stroked at the silky place she found that was driving Grey wild. She smiled as Grey screamed her name and clamped tightly around her fingers.

"I've missed you so much, Boone Fairway."

"I've missed you, too, baby."

"Now lay back and let me at you!"

Boone did as she was instructed. She rolled onto her back and spread her legs, watching Grey watch her and getting hotter by the minute.

Grey kissed Boone hard on the mouth, her hand tracing lovingly over her body. She sucked on an earlobe and nibbled her neck.

Boone was a bundle of nerves, all tense, waiting for the release she knew would come eventually. She watched as Grey kissed down her chest and saw her close her eyes as she drew her nipple in her mouth. Boone was awash with emotions as she watched the pleasure play across Grey's face.

Grey sucked on one nipple, then the other before continuing kissing down Boone's body. She left love bites on Boone's belly as she made her way to her center. She finally climbed between Boone's legs and Boone's whole body shuddered when she felt Grey's tongue brush lightly over her clit.

She felt Grey's fingers playing around her opening and she arched her back, begging her to enter. Grey finally did and Boone felt the sense of fullness that she craved.

Grey twisted and turned her hand inside Boone while she licked and sucked at her clit. Boone placed her hand on the back of Grey's head, urging her on. She bucked against her, oblivious to everything save the sensations she was feeling. She finally felt the tension break apart as the orgasms washed over her again and again.

Boone pulled Grey next to her and held her close.

"That was fantastic," Boone said.

"Yes, it was."

"Did you mean what you said? Earlier, I mean?"

"Did you?"

"I did."

"So, did I."

Boone pulled Grey closer and kissed the top of her head. Life was looking up.

CHAPTER SIXTEEN

Monday evening, Boone hurried out of the bar after happy hour. She hadn't seen Tanner since the incident at the shelter, and she and Grey had been spending all their time together. But today was special, as it was Phoebe's first day back to work. She couldn't wait to get to the shelter to see how it had gone.

She let herself into the office and was greeted with a passionate kiss from Grey.

"Hey now," Boone said. "Save some of that for later."

"I have plenty for you. You should know that."

Boone smiled.

"So, is Phoebe back from work yet?"

"She is."

"Do you know how it went?"

"Why don't you ask her?"

"I will."

Boone found Phoebe in the common room, watching TV.

"How was your day?"

"It was amazing! It was almost like I'd never missed a day. They all welcomed me back and had plenty of work for me to do."

"Good. I'm so happy to hear that."

"I love my job, Boone. And I'm glad they understand

my situation. They were all nice about me being away, but no one was sickeningly sweet over it. They made me feel comfortable."

"That's awesome, Phoebs."

"I know. And since I have that job, I'll be able to afford to move out of here sometime. I'll finally be on my own."

"That's fantastic. You've come so far. I'm so proud of you."

"I couldn't have done it without you, though. I'm really grateful for all you've done for me."

"All I did was turn you on to this place. The rest has been you and Grey and her staff."

"But you supported and encouraged me every step of the way. For that I thank you."

"You're welcome. How could I not? I knew you deserved the very best life had to offer. And you're going to get it. That's awesome."

"Will you stay for dinner tonight? I want to celebrate."

"Why not let Grey and I take you out for dinner? It may be a bit unconventional, but I'd like to do that for you."

"Sure, if Grey says it's okay."

"I'll go ask."

Boone found Grey in the office, wrapping up her day.

"So, I may have just broken a rule," Boone said.

"What did you do?"

"I just invited Phoebe to dinner with us tonight."

"How is that breaking a rule?"

"I didn't know how you'd feel about having dinner with a resident outside the shelter."

"She's not just a resident," Grey said. "Surely you know that."

"I was hoping you'd say that."

Grey's mood was light as she drove them to a little, out-of-the-way steak house. She listened to Boone and Phoebe chat away and felt blessed at the life she had.

Dinner was delicious, with Boone footing the bill. They enjoyed wine and a great meal and Phoebe was the most relaxed Grey had ever seen her.

"Happiness looks good on you, Phoebs," she said.

"Thanks. I feel great. I know my life is on the right path finally. I'm sorry I ever met Tanner Fairway. But then, I guess if I'd never met him, I wouldn't know you, would I?"

"No, but then you'd have been a lot better off. But you're on your way now."

"Yes, I am."

After dinner, they dropped Phoebe back at the shelter and Boone and Grey headed back to Grey's place.

"That was very nice of you, taking Phoebe out," Grey said.

"It's the least I could do for her. She's come so far in such a short amount of time. And thank you for joining us. Like I said, I know it's not protocol, but I think it helped validate her."

"I do, too. And I was happy to go. More time with you, and I do think Phoebe is an extraordinary woman."

"Do you think she'll be able to get out of there and live on her own?"

"I do."

"That's great."

"Now, isn't there something you'd rather do than talk about Phoebe?" Grey asked, slipping out of her clothes.

"Oh yeah," Boone said. "Definitely."

Grey saw Boone's eyes darken and felt her insides melt. She wanted Boone desperately, perhaps more than ever before, if that was possible. She watched Boone's gaze roam over her body and felt herself flush with her desire.

"Take me now, Boone," she said.

"Gladly."

Boone sat Grey on the couch and knelt between her legs. She buried her face against her, licking and tasting every inch of her. Grey felt her tongue deep inside her as her thumbs teased her clit.

"Oh God, baby, what you do to me," Grey said. She held Boone's head in place and rotated her hips to make her hit all the spots she needed. She felt wanton as she moved against her, but it felt so good she couldn't stop.

"Oh, Boone. Holy shit, Boone," she cried as she climaxed.

"Let's get to bed," Boone said.

Grey felt Boone's gaze burning into her as she led the way down the hallway. She turned and quickly undressed Boone. She leaned into her, feeling the warmth of her body searing her.

"You're so hot," Grey said. "You have the most amazing body."

"Yours isn't so bad, either."

"Kiss me, Boone."

Boone kissed her and Grey opened her mouth, welcoming her tongue. Boone felt soft, yet powerful at the same time. Grey swooned against her, her breasts pressing into Boone's firmness. She felt her nipples pucker. She needed Boone again.

She lay back on the bed and pulled Boone on top of her. She spread her legs to make room for Boone's knee, which she ground into as they continued to kiss. She was breathless when the kiss ended, but still pulled Boone back to her for more. She was lost in her desire, needing to feel Boone all over.

Boone responded to Grey's need completely. She cupped her face and matched the passion in her kiss. She released her grip and ran her hand the length of her body. Grey arched, urging her on, needing her touch.

Boone finally settled her hand between Grey's legs and Grey gasped at the touch. She loved how Boone knew exactly what to do to please her. She moved against Boone, driving her harder and deeper.

Grey wrapped her arms around Boone, pulling her whole body against her as she rode her hand to an explosive orgasm.

"My baby needed that," Boone said.

"God yes, I did."

"You were amazing."

"That was all you." Grey didn't know how Boone could possibly think she'd had anything to do with it. "You're an amazing lover."

"We're good together. That's for sure."

"Now it's your turn." Grey rolled Boone onto her back and climbed between her legs. She loved the flavors that were Boone. She was salty and sweet and delicious. She devoured every inch of her, licking and sucking everything she could reach. She focused her mouth on Boone's clit and buried her fingers inside. She felt Boone rising into her and knew she was close.

Grey felt her own orgasm building inside her. The excitement of pleasing Boone was that powerful. She heard Boone cry out just as her own climax exploded within her and they rode the waves together.

❖

Boone left work right after lunch the next day. She drove out to the shelter, where she found Cecilia alone in the office.

"Hi, Cecilia. Do you happen to know where Grey is?"

"I think she's in with her last patient of the day."

"Oh good. I'm glad it's a light day for her."

"Are you surprising her with something?" Cecilia asked.

"Sort of. It's more for Phoebe, but I was hoping Grey would join me."

"I think her afternoon is free, so if you want to make yourself comfortable, she should be out soon."

Boone relaxed on the love seat in the office and waited. Grey walked in ten minutes later, and Boone's breath caught at the sight of her. She was amazed at the effect Grey had on her. She looked stunning in her gray skirt and red blouse. She looked every bit the professional she was, but her sexiness couldn't be contained, even in business attire.

"Well, hello there," Grey said. "To what do I owe this pleasure?"

"I was hoping to steal you away for a few hours. I want to do something for Phoebe, but I need your help."

"How can I help?"

"If you're free for a few hours, come with me and find out."

"I'm free, right, Cecilia?"

"Yes, ma'am."

"Great. So what do I need to take with me?"

"Just your purse."

"Fair enough."

They walked out to Boone's truck.

"So, are you going to tell me where we're going?"

"You'll see soon enough."

Boone drove them through town until they reached the suburbs. She navigated them through until she arrived at a Nissan dealership.

She pulled in.

"Boone, you can't be serious."

"About what?"

"Are you thinking of buying Phoebe a car?"

"I am. Why not? Think about it. In her old beater, Tanner would instantly recognize her if he saw her. But if she's in a different car, she'd be practically invisible to him."

"That's true, but buying her a car?"

"She can't afford one on her own."

"Wow. Your generosity never ceases to amaze me."

"Come on."

They searched the lot until they found an older model that was still in good shape. They took it for a test drive.

"It handles really well. And it's in so much better shape than that thing she drives now," Boone said.

"Plus it's more reliable."

"So, we agree. We're buying this one."

"I still can't believe you're doing this for her."

"I have to. I need to do whatever I can to keep her safe."

"You know, Boone. I think you need to start forgiving yourself. What happened wasn't your fault even though Tanner is your brother."

Boone didn't know what to say. She didn't blame herself for what happened. She didn't blame herself for being related to Tanner. She hated him and hated that he was her brother, but didn't consider it her fault.

"Boone?"

"Huh? Oh, yeah. I don't blame myself, Grey."

"I think you do. And I think you need to let that go."

"Look. Tanner's an asshole. And, yeah, he's my brother, but we can't choose our blood relatives. I just have always thought that Phoebe is a sweetheart who deserves better. And if I can help keep Tanner away from her in any way, I will."

"Okay. If you say so."

"I do. Why don't you take my truck back to the shelter and I'll stay and get all the paperwork taken care of?"

Boone watched Grey take off and was still a little miffed at her for thinking she blamed herself, but cleared her head as she entered the finance office to deal with the car.

Two hours later, Boone drove off the lot and back to the shelter. She arrived before Phoebe got home from work and parked the car next to her truck. She went in to find Grey working at her computer.

"I'm back," she said.

"I see. Listen, Boone. I didn't mean to upset you earlier."

"Let's not talk about it. I'm over it now."

"But we should talk about it."

"You're the eternal counselor, aren't you? But, babe, I don't need my head shrunk. I'm okay. And I have the means to do something nice that will help Phoebs, so I did. I didn't do it out of guilt. You need to trust me."

"I'm not trying to shrink your head, Boone."

"It feels to me like you are. Can we please let it go?"

"Fine. We will. But if you want to talk about it, know I'll listen and not judge, okay?"

"I'll keep that in mind." Boone fought to keep her mood upbeat. She just wanted Phoebe to get there. She knew she'd be excited and that would make everything worthwhile.

Her wish was granted a few minutes later when Phoebe walked in.

"Hey, Phoebs! How was work today?" Boone asked.

"It was brutal. But I'm not complaining. I love my job so I persevered. There was just a lot going on today. But I kept up pretty well, I think."

"Excellent. So, we have a little surprise for you."

"We?" Grey said. "Boone has a little surprise for you."

"You helped pick it out," Boone said.

"What is it?" Phoebe asked.

Boone held out the keys.

"What?" Phoebe stared at them.

"That car parked next to my truck out there is yours."

"Really?" Phoebe put her hands on her cheeks. "You bought me a car?"

"I did."

"Oh, Boone! Thank you. But I can't accept a car."

"Phoebe, think about it. Tanner knows your car. It's parked at work every day. That's not safe. And it's not like it's a brand-new car. It's an older model. But I really want you to have it. Now here."

Phoebe took the keys and Boone and Grey followed her outside.

Boone watched as Phoebe took in the white Sentra parked there. Phoebe turned around and hugged her.

"Thank you so much!"

"You're very welcome. Go ahead. Take it for a spin."

"You two will come with me, right?"

They all climbed in and Phoebe drove around the neighborhood.

"This car is so fancy compared to mine."

"Well, I'll be taking your car and selling it tomorrow," Boone said. "So stop thinking of it as yours. This is yours now."

"Thank you again, Boone. This is so generous."

"I want you to be safe, Phoebs. And this car is just one more step in that direction."

"You're the best," Phoebe said as they pulled back into the shelter's parking lot.

"I'm just happy to help." Boone turned to Grey. "Are you about done for the day?"

"I am. I'll follow you home?"

"Sounds good to me."

Grey followed Boone, loving the sight of her tall, strong

woman in her truck. She loved her so much, even more after seeing her generous display for Phoebe. Not many people would go that far to help someone they cared about, but Boone didn't think twice about it. It was refreshing to see someone like that and she was grateful that Boone was hers.

She parked behind her in the driveway and walked into her arms. Boone held her tight.

When they released, Grey looked into Boone's eyes.

"So, we're okay?"

"We're fine. Honest."

"Okay. I really am sorry I made you angry earlier."

"Babe, let's not go back there. I wasn't angry, really. More frustrated. I don't know how to make you understand that just because I love Phoebe, it doesn't mean I feel responsible. You're a counselor. You're supposed to be impartial. So, try to open your mind to believe what I'm saying, okay?"

Boone had a point. Grey nodded her head, conceding. Boone was a smart, together woman and Grey had to trust Boone knew her own feelings better than she did.

"Okay, sweetheart. I believe you."

"Good. Now let's get inside."

Grey took Boone's hand and walked inside with her. That simple contact made her feel happy and whole. She loved Boone's touch, sexual or not. She couldn't get enough of her. When she held her hand, she knew she was exactly where she belonged.

"Do you know how happy you make me?" she asked.

"I'm glad to hear I make you happy."

"I mean it. Do you honestly realize?"

Boone took Grey in her arms and gazed into her eyes.

"Baby, you make me so very happy. It's an honor to be able to do the same for you."

"Oh, Boone."

Boone lowered her head and Grey felt the familiar jump in her stomach. When their lips met, her legs went weak. She held on to Boone as the kiss heated up.

"Dear God, what you do to me," she said.

"If we keep this up, we'll be skipping dinner," Boone said. "And I'm starving."

Grey realized her stomach was grumbling, too. She hadn't eaten since breakfast.

"Let's make dinner," she said.

They worked together in the kitchen, making the meal, and Grey set the table while Boone served them. Grey was amazed anew at how easy everything was with Boone.

"I'm crazy about you," Grey said as they sat down.

"I'm crazy about you, too, baby."

"I mean it. I'm nuts about you."

"I know this. Are you okay, babe?"

"I'm fine. I'm better than fine. I'm great. I just love being with you."

"I admit, there's no place I'd rather be."

"I like hearing that."

"Eat up, because I plan to show you just how much I care about you."

When the dinner dishes were done, Boone took Grey's hand again and took her to the bedroom. They lay together on the bed with Boone stroking Grey's hair.

"You're so beautiful," she said.

"You're not so bad yourself."

"I love your hair."

Grey was beside herself. The tenderness was heating her up in so many ways. She had a warm contentedness filling her, as well as the familiar fire that came when she lay with Boone.

"I'm glad. That feels really good."

"Yeah? Good. I love stroking your hair. I love brushing it off your face so I can look into your beautiful eyes."

"You say the sweetest things."

"I mean every word I say."

Their lovemaking that night was gentle and tender. Gone was the urgency of the previous night. They took their time, with Boone guiding Grey to one climax after another.

Grey returned the favor, languishing between Boone's legs and slowly pleasing her. She was rewarded with several powerful orgasms. As usual, she was filled with pride at being the one to give Boone such pleasure.

"I love loving you," she said when she was in Boone's arms.

"You do it very well."

"Aw, thank you."

Boone kissed Grey, softly at first, then with more passion. She rolled over on top of her and Grey's heart raced, knowing what was coming.

Boone reached her hand between Grey's legs, finding her still wet.

"Oh my God, you feel amazing," Boone said.

Grey opened herself wider, welcoming Boone in. Boone slipped easily inside and stroked all the spots that took Grey closer to the edge. When Grey could stand it no longer, she crushed Boone to her and screamed her name, shocked as always at the intensity of the orgasms Boone elicited from her.

Boone pulled Grey to her again and Grey nestled against her chest, reveling in the closeness of her. She felt safe and protected in Boone's arms and was happy she was right where she needed to be.

Chapter Seventeen

Boone walked out of the kitchen after the lunch rush and noticed Tanner's truck in the parking lot before she found her lowlife brother sitting at the bar.

"Tanner. Long time no see."

"Not that long."

"How's it goin'?"

"I've been better. I can't believe that slut you're fucking had me arrested."

"Watch your language when you're talking about her, brother."

"I could call her a lot worse."

"But you won't," Boone said. "So, any word from Phoebe?"

"No, she's a fucking whore, too."

"Man, you're just all roses and sunshine today, aren't you?"

"Whatever. Just get me another beer."

"Yes, sir."

"And this one should be on you," Tanner said.

"Why's that?"

"It's the least you can do."

"You know, if you're that pissed at me, why do you even bother coming in here?"

"Because I know one of these days you're going to slip up and let on where Phoebe is."

"Tanner, I have no fucking clue where she is. She probably skipped town and is a million miles away by now. Have you checked in Florida for her?"

"Very funny. She has no money. She couldn't have gotten far."

"Are you sure?"

"I'm positive."

"Maybe her family helped her."

"Her dad's a good man," Tanner said. "He would have sent her packing right back to her husband where she belongs."

"I think she's probably found where she needs to be by now and you should just let it go."

"You'd like that, wouldn't you? I'm sure I'll see her car at your house sometime and then you'll finally be busted."

"What? Are you staking out my house or something?"

"I cruise by on occasion. Look, Boone. I know you're helping her. I just need to catch you in the act."

"I've got nothing to do with her. Why would I?"

"Because you'd like nothing better than to stick it to me, which helping her would certainly do," Tanner said.

"Why would I want to stick it to you? You're my brother."

"You're so full of shit. You've hated me since I was born."

"Again I ask, why do you even come in here, Tanner?"

"You're not always here, for starters."

"Fair enough."

"Okay. Look, I'm sorry I'm in such a foul mood today, but I'm still pissed you let the cops take me away that night."

"What could I do? It wasn't my house. And if it was, and you wouldn't leave, I might have done the same thing."

"I'm sure you would. But, hey, let's stop fighting. Sit. Have a beer with me."

Boone wanted nothing less than to spend any time with Tanner, but she figured it wouldn't hurt to soothe his bruised ego and have a beer with him. She grabbed two beers and handed one to him.

"So how's work?" she asked.

"It sucks."

"Why don't you find a different outfit to work for?"

"I should. My asshole boss is a slave driver. He pays us shit and expects the world from us."

Boone knew that wasn't true. Tanner made good money when he showed up for work. She didn't doubt that construction was a hard business, but Tanner had no other skills so couldn't get work in any other field.

"That bites," she said. "I'm sorry to hear that."

"Thanks. How's business here?"

"It's going pretty well. Football season is in full swing, which keeps us jumpin' on the weekends. And we still get a decent crowd every day for happy hour."

"Good. I'm glad to hear that."

She doubted he really was happy to hear that she was doing well, but at least he was trying to be nice. She wondered if he was getting ready to ask her for money.

"So no work for you this afternoon?" she asked.

"I should probably get back to it, actually." He downed his beer and stood.

"Well, thanks for stopping by."

"Yep. I'll see you."

She breathed a sigh of relief as she watched his truck pull out. She hated having him around and was always weary that he'd show up at the shelter again. She wished he would disappear into the sunset, but he was like a bad penny. She had to accept that he'd always be in her life.

Boone finished her beer and went home to swim some

laps to alleviate the tension that always came after a run-in with Tanner. She felt better after and soaked in the hot tub for a long while before showering and dressing to go see Phoebe.

She arrived at the shelter before Phoebe arrived back from work. Grey was with a resident, so Boone busied herself helping in the kitchen. She was there mashing potatoes when she felt arms wrap around her from behind and the feel of Grey's soft lips caress the back of her neck.

"Hey, you," Boone said.

"Hey yourself," Grey said. "You look mighty sexy in that apron, woman."

Boone turned and smiled into Grey's eyes. She kissed her softly. "I'm glad you think I'm sexy."

"Oh, honey. You have no idea."

"How was your day?" Boone asked.

"Come into my office and we can talk."

"Sounds good."

Boone followed Grey down the hallway, admiring, as always, the soft sway of her hips under her skirt.

They sat on the love seat, holding hands.

"My day was great. We got a new intake, unfortunately, but she seems to be a strong woman and I have faith she'll bounce back quickly."

"I hate that you have new residents. I mean, I know it's what keeps this place going, but I wish there was no need for a shelter like this."

"I know exactly what you mean. I wish there wasn't either. But I'm so happy that we have this place for the women who need it. How was your day?"

"Guess who showed up at the bar."

"Tanner?"

"Yep."

"I'm sorry, Boone."

"Yeah. He said a lot of unpleasant things about you. I was royally pissed at him."

"Well, that's to be expected. I was the one who had him hauled away by the police."

"Yeah, but he's such a douchebag. He hates women, you know? I mean, he really hates women. It's hard for me to fathom that depth of hatred."

"Is he still hell-bent on finding Phoebe?"

"Oh yeah," Boone said. "He hasn't let go of that at all. I so wish he'd accept she's gone and just move on. I even tried to tell him she'd probably left the area and he should leave it alone, but he won't."

They looked up when they heard someone in the doorway. They saw Phoebe watching them.

"Am I interrupting?" she asked.

"Not at all," Grey said.

"You two look so serious."

"It's all good," Boone said.

"You sure?" Phoebe asked.

"I'm sure."

"Tanner showed up at Boone's bar today," Grey said.

"I'm sorry," Phoebe said.

"Aren't we all? He tried to be nice after a while, but he's still an asshole."

"Don't I know it."

"I'm sorry, Phoebe. I wish he'd get out of all our lives," Boone said.

"So do I. But I don't worry about him finding me anymore. I feel safe and secure here and at work. Plus he doesn't know my new car. So I'm not afraid of him."

"Good for you," Grey said.

"I should go see if they need any more help in the kitchen." Boone stood.

"Nonsense," Phoebe said. "I'll go in there and help with dinner. You two go home and relax."

"I can't argue with that logic," Grey said.

"Neither can I."

Boone hugged Phoebe.

"It's really great to see you doing so well," she said.

"Thanks. The same goes for you."

Boone felt herself blush. She turned to Grey.

"Shall we?"

"We shall. I'll see you tomorrow, Phoebe."

"Have a good night," Phoebe said before leaving them alone.

"Where to?" Boone asked.

"You know what I have a hankering for?"

"Hard telling."

"I want a really good burger."

"I know just the place. We can go grab a burger and a beer. I know the owner, so we'll get a good deal and great service."

"The Boonies sounds great." Grey laughed.

Boone kept checking her rearview mirror, making sure Grey was behind her. She had no reason to worry, but it felt good to see her car there.

She pulled into the back lot and Grey parked next to her. They walked in the back door and Boone froze. Grey walked right into her back.

"What's wrong?"

"Tanner's here."

"Oh shit."

"Come on." Boone turned to leave. "Let's go somewhere else."

"No," Grey said. "We're not going to run away from him. This is your bar and you belong here."

"Yeah, but I don't want him to give you any grief."

"I'm a big girl," Grey said. "I can handle myself. Besides, you're with me, so I feel safe."

"If you're sure…"

"I'm positive. Now let's go."

Boone took Grey's hand and led her to the kitchen, where she wrote down their orders for the cook. She took her back behind the bar and grabbed a couple of iced teas.

"Well, well, well. Look who's here," Tanner said.

"Hey, Tanner. How was the rest of your day?" Boone tried to sound civil.

"Not as good as yours, I'm guessing. Did you just get laid?"

"That's really none of your business," Boone said.

"I'll take that as a yes. I've got to hand it to you, Boone. This new piece of yours is easy on the eyes."

"I warned you about talking about her that way."

"It's okay, Boone," Grey said. "I'm fine. Let's just go find a table."

"I can't believe you had me arrested, you whore."

Boone turned back to Tanner.

"Back off, Tanner. I'll have you kicked out of here if you don't zip it right now."

"You and her are just alike, aren't you?"

"Tanner…"

"Fine. I'll go back to playing pool. You two can fuck yourselves for all I care."

"He's so charming," Grey said when they were seated.

"I'm sorry you had to deal with him."

"His animosity toward me is warranted. I did have him arrested. And I will again if he ever shows up there again. But I doubt he will."

"I hope not."

The tension eased shortly thereafter when Tanner stumbled out the door and got in his truck.

"It's a wonder he doesn't have a dozen DUIs," Grey said as he drove off.

"I know." She motioned to the bartender, who came over to their table.

"What have I said about overserving people? Tanner was drunk as a skunk."

"He didn't get any from us. We refused to serve him. He only stayed for a game of pool then left. I promise you we didn't get him that way."

"Okay. Thanks." She turned to Grey. "Well, that's a relief anyway."

Their relief was short-lived. Tanner was back and got in Grey's face.

"Where's my wife?" he said.

"I don't know your wife," Grey said.

"Bullshit." He leaned closer. Boone could smell the whiskey on his breath. "No normal person has security guards posted around their house."

"I'm a paranoid person," she said.

"Fuck you. I'll give you something to be paranoid about," Tanner said and walked over to the pool table.

"You've got to kick him out," Grey said.

"He's not drinking," Boone said.

"If this has to come down to making you choose him or me, I'm willing to make you do that."

"That's not even a choice. You know you win."

"Prove it. Kick him out of here once and for all. I mean it, Boone."

Boone stared at Grey, and hoped she'd see some sign she

was messing with her. There was no such sign. Grey was dead serious.

"So eighty-six him?"

"Yes. Show me you're serious about cleaning up the bar."

Boone stood. Her stomach was in knots. She knew it was the right thing to do. She should have blocked Tanner from the bar years ago. But confrontation didn't come easy to her. Still, if she had to choose between Tanner and Grey, well, there really was no choice.

She crossed the bar to where Tanner was sitting on a stool waiting his turn at the pool table.

"Tanner, you're drunk," Boone said.

"I am not. Even though your pretty boy bartender says I'm too drunk to be served. I'm only shooting pool, not drinking. Now leave me alone."

"Look, I can't have you coming in here all drunk and belligerent all the time."

"Fuck you, little Miss Perfect."

"I'm serious, Tanner."

"So am I. Get the fuck out of my face."

"No, Tanner. You get out of my bar. Now."

"Make me."

"Tanner, you don't want me to make you. I tell you what. You sit here and I'll call you a cab and when it gets here, you go home."

"Bullshit. I don't need no cab and I'm not leaving."

Boone signaled both her bartenders to come over. They were both in their early twenties, around six feet tall and were lean, but muscular.

"Show Tanner to his car, please," Boone said.

Tanner stood, hatred in his eyes.

"Fuck you, bitch. I don't need your fucking bar anyway.

You can take your self-righteous ways and shove them up your ass. But don't think kicking me out of here will keep me away from you and your whore. I'm going to find my wife and I think you two know where she is."

Boone held her breath as she watched Tanner stumble back out to his truck. When he was gone, she walked back to the table.

"Well, that's done," Boone said.

"Thank you. I know it wasn't easy. He is your brother, after all."

"I don't know if that mattered to me. I hate the guy. I really do. I guess I just figured The Boonies was for anyone."

"I'm really happy you did that, Boone. I feel like you've shown me how much you've grown, how far you've come."

Boone tried to relax, but found it hard. The tension coursed through her. Grey must have noticed, as she stood behind Boone and rubbed her shoulders. Boone leaned into her.

"That feels good."

"Good. You just relax now."

"You're right," Boone said. "He's gone, so let's forget about him and get back to enjoying our evening."

They ate their burgers, watched some television, and Boone even let Grey win a game of pool. They were relaxed and happy as Grey followed Boone back to her place.

"That was so much fun," Grey said as they walked into the house.

"I'm glad you enjoyed it. It's not very upscale, but it's mine."

"Yes, it is. It's such a comfortable place to be. You should be proud of yourself for what you've made it."

"I actually am," Boone said. "I love that place."

"And it shows."

"I also love you," Boone said, taking Grey in her arms.

"And that shows, as well."

"Good. I never want you to doubt it."

"Maybe you should prove it to me right now," Grey said.

"I was thinking the same thing."

"Actually, you know what I'd like to do first?" Grey said.

"First? You mean I don't get to ravish you right now?"

"Nope. I'd like to relax in the hot tub with you first."

"That sounds wonderful."

Boone poured them each a glass of wine and they donned thick robes to walk out to the hot tub. Boone stood back and watched as Grey slipped out of her robe and stepped into the water. She watched the warm water reach up and caress her softest spots until the bubbles hid them from her view. She wanted Grey more than ever and quickly stripped off her own robe to join her.

She sat next to Grey and wrapped an arm around her, pulling her close. The night air had just enough chill to add to the excitement of the hot tub. She was feeling the need to take Grey right there, but knew Grey just wanted a nice soak.

"This feels amazing," Grey said, leaning her head back and looking at the stars. "And look at all the stars you can see here. I'd think the city lights would be too bright to see them."

"Everything is beautiful tonight," Boone said. She ran her hand along the underside of one of Grey's breasts.

"You say the sweetest things."

"You have the sweetest things." She closed her hand over the breast. "I just can't get enough of you."

"Nor I you." She turned her head and pulled Boone to her for a kiss. It was a long, sensual kiss, their tongues slowly teasing each other.

"You are such a good kisser," Boone said.

"We kiss very well together, that's for sure."

"That we do." Boone kissed her again, another lazy kiss that hinted at so much more to come.

"How long are we staying out here?" Boone asked, a jumble of hormones.

"Just a little while longer. I promise to make it worth your while.

"I don't doubt that you will."

They relaxed in the water, the jets gently easing any tension out of their bodies. Boone remained alert, however, awaiting the go sign from Grey.

She finally felt Grey's hand on her thigh.

"Baby, I feel so good. Thank you for this. It was just what I needed."

"I know what else you need," Boone said.

"Mm. So do I."

She eased her hand up Boone's leg until it teased where her legs joined.

"Baby, you're playing with fire."

"I like your fire. I want to play with it all the time." She pried Boone's legs apart and slid her hand between them. "I love your fire."

Boone leaned her head back and closed her eyes. Grey's touch was superb. She knew exactly what to do and when to do it. Boone had been with many women before, but none were as skilled at loving her as Grey was instinctively. She felt her fingers touching all her sensitive spots and spread her legs wider, craving more.

Grey worked lovingly and tirelessly as Boone teetered closer and closer to the brink, finally catapulting over into an overwhelming orgasm.

"That was fantastic," Boone said when she finally caught her breath. "Fucking amazing."

"Good. Let's get inside and dry off so you can return the favor."

They lay together on the bed, Boone propped up on an elbow looking down at Grey.

"You're so beautiful. You take my breath away. I've never been in love like this before."

She watched the blush start on Grey's chest and work its way to her cheeks.

"It's true. You don't need to be embarrassed."

"Who said I was embarrassed?"

"I can see your whole body blush," Boone said.

"Oh, yeah. You do have an unfair advantage there."

Boone ran her hand over Grey's breasts, watching her nipples pucker. She moved so one nipple poked into her palm.

"I love your nipples."

"They certainly enjoy you."

"I'm glad." She bent and took a nipple in her mouth, drawing it deep. She flicked the tip of it with her tongue and felt Grey squirm.

"You like that, huh?"

"Oh, dear God."

She bent to take the other one as she skimmed her hand down Grey's body and settled it between her legs.

"I love how you're always ready for me."

"Always. I'm always ready for you to take me."

"You feel so good down there." She moved her fingers inside her and watched as Grey closed her eyes.

"That feels so good," Grey said.

"Yeah? You like that?" Boone withdrew her fingers and plunged them in again. She twisted her hand, pressing into Grey as she did.

"Oh yeah, Boone. Oh yes, please."

Boone continued to move around inside Grey, stroking

her with her fingers until she felt the tremors begin. She loved her harder and faster until Grey finally cried out and let the climax overtake her.

Boone pulled Grey into her arms and held her close, feeling her heart rate slow back to normal.

"I love it when you hold me like this," Grey said. "I feel so safe in your arms."

"Baby?"

"Hmm?"

"You've mentioned how I make you feel safe a couple of times today. Do you not feel safe generally as a rule?"

Grey propped herself up and looked at Boone.

"It's not that I don't feel safe usually. I don't live in a state of fear or anything. But with you, I feel protected and safe and secure. It's just a really nice feeling."

"Okay. I just don't like the idea of you ever not feeling safe."

"No worries. It's just that it's amplified in your arms."

"Good. Because you're always safe with me."

"I know this, Boone."

Boone pulled her close again and held her as they drifted off to sleep.

EPILOGUE

Spring had sprung in the Pacific Northwest, bringing with it warmer days and more sunshine. Boone woke one morning feeling particularly good about life. It was a big day for everyone and she could feel it in her bones. The warm morning air drifted through the open window and blew over her like a lover's breath. It stirred the fire already burning inside her.

She rolled over and kissed Grey's shoulder, loving the feel of her soft skin beneath her lips. Grey stirred slightly, but remained asleep. Boone almost felt guilty for wanting to wake her, but her needs were great and only Grey could satisfy them. She kissed her again and ran her hand down her naked back, cupping the smooth curves of her hips.

"Mm." Grey rolled over and stretched. "Someone woke up in a mood."

"I did indeed." Boone kissed her shoulder again and nuzzled her neck. "You looked too good lying there for me not to have my way with you."

"You can always have your way with me."

"I feel bad for waking you up, though."

"No, you don't." Grey laughed. "And I certainly don't."

Grey took Boone's hand. She spread her legs and placed Boone's hand between them.

"Ah," she said. "That's where you belong."

Boone made love to Grey quickly and passionately, her desire for her apparent in every motion. She took Grey to one orgasm after another until Grey finally tapped her shoulder.

"No more," she whispered. "No more."

Boone laughed as she looked down on the satiated Grey.

"You sure you've had enough?"

"I'm positive."

Grey curled up against Boone and fell right back to sleep. Boone smiled at the feel of Grey's body against her, content to have her in her life.

They woke an hour later. Grey sat straight up in bed.

"Oh my God. What time is it?"

"It's only ten o'clock. Relax. We have plenty of time."

Grey fell back against her pillow.

"Thank God. It feels later."

"Nope. I wouldn't have let us oversleep. Today's a big day."

"It really is. I'm so excited."

"Me, too. You ready to hit the shower?"

"I am."

Grey followed Boone down the hall to the bathroom. Boone turned on both showerheads, then stood back to let Grey enter. She loved to watch the water cascading over Grey's body and felt the familiar stirring deep inside.

Grey apparently was feeling it too, as she turned and wrapped her arms around Boone as soon as Boone entered the shower. They kissed briefly before Grey bent to take one of Boone's nipples in her mouth.

Boone braced herself against the wall, not trusting her legs to keep her upright.

Grey kissed down Boone's torso until she knelt between

her legs. Boone felt her tongue working its magic and let herself go. The climax was almost immediate.

"You're so easy," Grey teased, lathering her loofah.

"Hey now. At least I'm not a pillow queen."

"Is that what I am?" Grey laughed.

"You sure were this morning."

"And I deserve to be."

"So you do." Boone pulled Grey to her and washed her back, reveling in the feel of her nipples poking her. She brought her washcloth around to the front of her and gently washed her breasts, before dipping it between her legs.

"Why did I bother with my loofah?" Grey asked.

"I don't know. You had to know I was going to wash you. Any chance I get to enjoy that body, I'm going to take."

"Well, now it's my turn." She scrubbed Boone then they rinsed off, with Boone never taking her eyes off Grey's lithe body under her showerhead.

They dried off and dressed and were finally ready to start their day.

"We're supposed to be there at one, right?" Boone said.

"Yep. We need to hit the store first."

"Yes, we do."

They drove to the store and bought burgers and hot dogs and buns. Then they drove to The Boonies and Boone ran inside to pick up a couple cases of beer.

"Okay. Do we know how to get there?" Grey asked when Boone was back in the truck.

"We have GPS."

They drove through the suburbs to a small apartment complex.

"This looks like the place," Boone said.

They found a place to park and followed the voices around

to a pool area. There they saw many familiar faces, mostly residents of the shelter, past and present. They were able to pick Phoebe out of the crowd and she waved them over.

"I'm so glad you two could make it," Phoebe said.

"We wouldn't have missed this for anything," Boone said. "Where should we put this stuff?"

"Come on in. I'll show you around."

They followed her into a studio apartment. It was small, but well furnished.

"This is really cute, Phoebe," Grey said.

"Thanks," Phoebe said. "And it's all mine!"

"That's the best part of it," Boone said. "I'm so proud of you."

"Thank you. I couldn't have done it without the two of you."

"Don't play down your part," Grey said. "You were instrumental in moving on with your life and getting your own place."

"I am so thrilled to have this," Phoebe said. "I love having a place of my own."

Boone thought Phoebe looked amazing. She was wearing a shirt over her bathing suit, and she looked relaxed and at ease. More so than she'd ever seen her.

"Did you bring your suits with you?" Phoebe asked.

"We did."

"Well, get changed and come on out and join the party."

"Okay, we'll meet you there," Boone said.

They stepped into the small bathroom and stripped out of their clothes.

"Come here," Boone whispered.

"Boone! Not now."

"Oh yeah. Now."

She ran her hands over Grey's naked body, bringing one to rest between her legs. She found her wet and ready.

"I think someone wants this as bad as I do."

"I can't believe you."

"I want you. I always want you. I can't help it."

She rubbed Grey's swollen clit briefly and Grey bit into her shoulder to keep from crying out.

They finished changing and joined the party. Grey mingled with the residents while Boone manned the grill. She barbecued the hot dogs and burgers and handed out beers to people who stopped by. It was great to see all the women there. So many of them were success stories and it made her feel good to see the women Grey had helped over the years.

"How you doing?" Grey walked over and wrapped her arms around Boone.

"I'm doing great. How are you?"

"I'm having so much fun."

"That's awesome. Babe, I'm so proud of you. I see all these women and it makes my heart swell with pride that you've had a hand in them getting their lives on track."

"Thank you. That's very sweet of you to say."

"It's true, baby. I'm so proud you're mine."

They kissed, long and slow, oblivious to the crowd around them.

"I love you," Grey said.

"I love you."

"Hey, you two," Phoebe said. "The party's kind of breaking up. Did you want to go get something to drink or something?"

"I think we'll take a rain check," Boone said. "We need to get home."

"I understand." Phoebe winked.

They hugged good-bye.

"I'm so proud of you," Boone said again.

"Thank you. Thanks to both of you."

"Keep up the good work, Phoebe," Grey said.

"I will."

Boone took Grey's hand and led her to her truck. She pressed her against the door and kissed her hard on the mouth, her hands roaming over her body.

"God, I love you."

"Let's get home," Grey said.

They drove off into the sunset, knowing what treats were in store for them at home.

Please turn the page for an exciting sneak peek of MJ Williamz's book SUMMER PASSION coming in November 2015!

Summer Passion

"Cut!" the director yelled. "That's a wrap. Good job, everyone."

Jean Sanders walked off the set and into her dressing room. She felt good about the scenes they had shot that day. She sat down and lit a cigarette, inhaling deeply. While there were certain things about being America's Sweetheart that were draining, having her own private dressing room was certainly not one of them.

She was happy with the new movie they were filming. It wasn't a musical or a western, which were so prevalent right then. It was a heart-wrenching movie about a woman struggling to overcome the loss of her husband during the war. She thought she was playing the part well.

Her thoughts were interrupted by a knock on her door.

"Come."

"Miss Sanders, Mr. Duvall has invited you to dinner," one of the stagehands said. David Duvall was the director. He was queer as a three-dollar bill, so she knew it was safe to go out with him. And they often dined together. She was glad she hadn't unrolled her hair yet.

"Tell him I'll be out in twenty minutes."

She washed off the thick makeup she wore for the cameras and skillfully applied her everyday makeup. She finished by applying the deep red lipstick on her lips and stood. She slipped out of her costume and into a nice dress for dinner. She knew David wanted to show her off and would only take her to an upscale restaurant.

Jean checked herself out in the mirror and, satisfied, stepped onto the set again to find David sitting in his chair waiting for her.

"My darling Jean, you look radiant."

"Thank you, David."

"I thought we'd have Italian tonight. Barichelli's sound good to you?"

"Sounds delicious. I'm famished."

It was a pleasant Hollywood evening. The air was cool but not chilly and Jean was comfortable in her dress. They drove off the set and to the Sunset Strip, the section of Hollywood where people went to see and be seen.

David handed his keys to the valet, then helped Jean out of the car.

"You sure know how to make an exit," he said. "You've got the shapeliest legs in the business."

"Why, David, you'll make me blush."

"I don't think that's possible."

She took his arm and smiled as the cameras around them flashed and took their picture. She was used to it. And she was used to the rumors linking her with David. It worked for both of them, so they let the gossips wag their tongues.

They managed to get inside the restaurant, where David slipped the maître d' a twenty dollar bill to be seated soon. It worked and soon they were at a table in the center of the restaurant. If it was privacy they wanted, they would have found a different spot. Several times during the meal, people came up and asked Jean for her autograph, which she graciously provided.

"Your public loves you," David said.

"Yes, they do. And they will love me even more once *Scars of the Heart* comes out."

"Isn't it a masterpiece of a movie? I've no doubt it'll be a smash."

"Well, tomorrow is another early day on the set," Jean said. "You should probably get me home."

"Yes, dear. I'll drop you off. And, of course, I'll send a car for you in the morning."

"Thank you."

They drove to Jean's estate several miles outside of town. It was a lovely, rambling house surrounded by well-kept gardens in the middle of an orange grove.

"As always, it was a pleasure, my dear."

"Yes, it was, David. Thank you again. I'll see you tomorrow."

She got out of the car and let herself in her front door.

"I was beginning to wonder if you were ever coming home," said a woman sitting on a white leather chair.

"Betty. I didn't realize you were still here."

Betty was Jean's longtime maid. She sat in her maid uniform with her legs stretched out before her, clad in fishnet stockings. The high heels she had on clearly indicated she wasn't there to clean the house.

"I took a shower after I finished and thought I'd wait and see what kind of mood you were in when you got home."

Jean walked behind Betty and lightly dragged her fingers along one side of her neck while she nuzzled the other side.

"Mmm. You smell good."

"I used your favorite powder."

"My Betty is in a mood tonight, aren't you?"

"Well, I wanted to please you, Ms. Sanders."

"And be pleased by me, perhaps?"

Jean watched the flush pass over Betty. She loved knowing Betty was so anxious for her. She always enjoyed their playtime.

She slid her hand down the front of Betty's maid uniform and closed it on a full breast.

"Oh, Betty. You were made for pleasure. Stand up for me."

Betty did as she was told. Jean walked around her, checking her out.

"Take off that dress," she said.

Betty started to unbutton it and Jean reached out and grabbed her hand.

"Slowly."

Betty slowed and unbuttoned her dress, letting it slip off her shoulders and land in a heap on the floor.

Jean walked around her again, admiring her full figure. She was sexy as hell in her thigh-high stockings. She was glad she hadn't bothered with panties. They were a waste of time, and Jean seldom wore them herself.

She stood in front of Betty, staring into her eyes. She loved the passion she saw burning there.

"Do you want me, Betty?"

"Oh, yes."

Jean kissed her then, a soft, light kiss.

"You taste good. You taste like wine. Did you have some of my wine?"

"Just a glass."

"Good. I don't want you to be numb. I want you alert to feel everything."

"I want that, too."

Jean put one hand behind Betty's head and pulled her to her, kissing her passionately on the mouth. Betty's mouth opened immediately, and Jean thrust her tongue inside while she slipped her other hand between Betty's legs to feel how wet and ready she was for her. She plunged her fingers inside as she continued to move her tongue in her mouth.

She felt Betty moan into her mouth as she neared her climax. She continued to work her fingers until Betty collapsed against her.

"Is that what you needed?" Jean asked.

"Oh, yes."

Jean took her hand and led her to the couch. She laid her back and placed one leg over the back of the couch. She climbed between her legs and lapped up the evidence of her orgasm. She continued to lick every inch of her, spending more time on her clit, which she knew to be hypersensitive. In no time at all, Betty was calling out her name.

"May I please you now, Ms. Sanders?" Betty asked.

"Not tonight. I have an early call."

"Okay." Betty was clearly disappointed.

"I'm sorry I got home so late. Had I known you were waiting, perhaps I would have forgone dinner out. But you know I need to be seen out and about on occasion."

"I understand. I'll get dressed and see myself out. Thank you, though. I had a swell time."

"As did I."

She kissed her good night and went to her room.

She slipped out of her clothes and climbed between her silky-soft sheets. The feel of the fabric on her bare skin did little to cool the heat she was feeling after fucking Betty. She reached between her legs and found her clit swollen and slick. She should have let Betty take care of her, but she had to get up early, and it wouldn't do to show up on the set with dark circles under her eyes. Still, she couldn't sleep and felt that a clit that hard shouldn't be wasted.

She closed her eyes and thought about Dorothy Martin,

the woman she costarred with in her last movie. Her dark eyes and sensual smile had teased Jean for months. She imagined Dorothy's long fingers caressing her as she stroked between her legs. She fantasized about playing with Dorothy's voluptuous breasts as she pleased herself. As everything she saw in her mind's eye played out, Jean brought herself to a powerful orgasm.

Filming went well for the next few weeks, and soon *Scars of the Heart* was a wrap. Jean threw a tremendous party at her estate. All the stars were there, including Dorothy Martin. Jean did her best to charm the cold woman, to no avail. She was a frustrated mess as she wandered the grounds seeing women making out with each other and men doing the same. She needed to find a woman to bed.

A woman she didn't know approached her.

"Ms. Sanders? Jean Sanders? Oh my God. I can't believe it's really you."

"Who else would it be? It's my house."

"I know. But there are so many people here. I never dreamed I'd actually meet you."

Jean was intrigued. The young woman was clearly a fan. But she was a very attractive fan. Which made it very tempting for Jean to attempt to seduce her. But she couldn't take a chance. Her sexuality had to stay out of the public's eye.

"Well, it's a pleasure to meet you," Jean said.

"The pleasure is mine. I'm thrilled to meet you."

"Thank you. That's very nice of you to say."

"I know it's not right to ask for an autograph at a party like this…" the woman said.

"How did you hear about this party?" Jean wondered how a fan had gotten in to the party.

"I came with Dorothy Martin."

"You did?" Jean was intrigued.

"Yes. You might say I'm her date."

"Date, date?"

"Well, I don't know how to answer that."

"Answer it honestly," Jean said. "You can tell me. What do you think I am? An old fuddy-duddy?"

"I should probably go find Dorothy."

"Okay. Well, again, it was nice meeting you."

"Nice meeting you, too."

Jean watched the woman walk off and enjoyed the view.

Her curiosity and libido piqued, she wandered back to the house to see what was happening there. People were dancing in the ballroom. Others were relaxing in the sitting rooms. Everyone seemed to be having fun.

She saw Betty serving her guests and watched as several women made passes at her. She smiled. She knew Betty was probably more than they could handle. She also knew Betty knew she was working at the moment, so every woman was off-limits.

The sexual mood of the party did nothing to cool her needs. Hollywood was a place where lesbians had to be secretive, but at her parties, everyone was free. If only she could find someone to be free with.

Jean felt the gaze on her before she noticed the brunette watching her from across the room. She looked vaguely familiar with green eyes that called to Jean. Where did she know her from? She tried to remember before she crossed the room. She needn't have worried. The woman approached her as well.

"Hello, Jean. It's good to see you again."

Jean panicked. So she did know the woman. But how?

"You don't remember me," the woman said. "I don't blame you. I was an extra on the set of *Nights in Miami*. You were always so nice to me. I appreciated that."

"Of course! That's how I know you. I knew you looked familiar. How goes the career?"

"I've been getting bigger and bigger parts lately. I'm hoping to be famous like you someday."

"Forgive me," Jean said, "But your name escapes me."

"Oh, I'm sorry. My name is Margaret. But you can call me Maggie."

"It's good to see you again, Maggie." Jean searched for something to say. Maggie's long brown hair and piercing green eyes had Jean hoping for more than a casual conversation with her. "Can I get you something to drink?"

"I'd love a martini."

"Done. Would you like to come with me or wait for me here?"

"I'll join you, if you don't mind."

"I don't mind at all."

They walked back to the quiet area that was Jean's bar.

"So, Maggie, do you have a last name?"

"Cranston."

"Excellent. I hope to see 'Margaret Cranston' in big lights some day."

"Thank you. You have been my idol for years. I hope I make it like you have."

"Well, it sounds like you're on your way. Bigger parts are always a good thing. Tell me, what kind of roles are you looking for?"

"The usual…a romantic lead. I'm not that interested in horror movies. I like good, old-fashioned romances."

Jean nodded.

"Not to say I wouldn't take a role like that if it came along. But that's not where my heart lies."

"I understand. Let's take this conversation outside."

Jean took Maggie's hand and led her into her small,

personal garden. No one else was allowed there, so they had plenty of privacy.

"So where did you get your training, Maggie?"

"I went to Bryn Mawr."

"That's a good school."

"I also did some stock work. I think I'm proving myself a good actress."

"You did good work on *Miami*, as I recall. I'm sure you're making a name for yourself."

"Thank you. That means the world to me."

"And what do you do in your free time? What are some of your interests?"

"I like to read and, of course, practice my acting."

"What do you like to read?"

"I like Elizabeth Bishop and Radclyffe Hall."

Jean understood exactly what Maggie was saying. She was safe. She, too, was a lesbian, and Jean could relax and be free with her.

"I've read Hall as well. It was fairly depressing."

"Yes. But it was so nice to read about people like me. Like us?"

"Yes. Like us."

Maggie smiled. Her whole face lit up. Her eyes sparkled. Jean could see the want in them.

"Would you like another drink?" Jean asked.

"Sure."

They made their way back into the house. When Jean took Maggie's glass from her, their fingers touched and Jean felt the shock to her core. She knew she would have to have Maggie, and soon.

Drinks in hand, they meandered back to the garden.

"Can I show you around?" Jean asked.

"I'd like that."

Jean led her past the rosebushes and various other plants that made up her lush garden. When they were out of sight of the house, Jean moved nearer to Maggie.

"I like you, Maggie Cranston."

"I like you, too, Jean."

Jean closed the distance between them. She stood taller than Maggie and looked into her eyes. The desire she saw matched hers. She slowly lowered her mouth until it was just inches from Maggie's.

"You're beautiful," Jean whispered.

She watched Maggie's eyes close. She brushed her lips lightly over Maggie's. They were soft and tasted faintly of martini. She pulled away.

"That was nice," she said.

"Very."

Jean kissed her again, more passionately this time. She ran her tongue over Maggie's lips and they parted, allowing her entry. Her mouth was warm and moist, much as she knew she'd find other parts. Her legs went weak as the kiss deepened.

"Come up to my room?" Jean whispered hoarsely.

"Lead the way."

Jean led Maggie in a secret entrance to avoid curious stares. She took her upstairs to her room. The big four-poster bed beckoned her. She kissed Maggie again, hard and powerfully, claiming her as her own.

As they kissed, Jean deftly unbuttoned Maggie's blouse. She slid it off her shoulders and down to the floor. The soft skin beneath the silky bra called to her. It teased her to the point of dizziness.

Light-headed, she caressed the small mounds. She bent to kiss one, then the other.

"Please," Maggie murmured. "Get this off me."

Jean reached around behind her and unhooked her bra.

She tossed it to the floor, then held both breasts in her hands. She ran her thumbs over the pert nipples and they stood hard under her touch. She lowered her head and licked one, feeling it harden even more. She sucked it deep in her mouth and felt the nipple pressed against the roof of her mouth.

Maggie held her head in place as she mewled. Jean was excited at the sounds she made. But she needed more. Much more.

While she continued to suck, Jean found the button and zipper to Maggie's skirt, and soon it joined the other clothes on the floor.

"My God, you're beautiful," Jean breathed.

She watched as the blush crept over every inch of Maggie. Her desire flared. She ran her hand down Maggie's backside and felt the satin fabric of her panties against her skin. She slipped her fingers inside the waistband and felt Maggie's stomach ripple in response. She knew Maggie was ripe for the picking and couldn't wait to taste her fruit.

Jean slid Maggie's panties off and watched her shapely legs as she stepped out of them. She eased her back on the bed. When she climbed on top, Maggie worked quickly to strip her clothes. Skin to skin, Jean kissed Maggie again, this time with all the pent-up passion she had. She felt every inch of Maggie against her, her heated flesh spurring her on.

They continued kissing as they rubbed against each other. Jean finally broke the kiss and worked her way lower, once again taking a nipple in her mouth. She sucked on it, playfully at first, then in earnest. She was lost in the sensation of the hard nub in her mouth and the puckered areola against her lips.

She moved her hand to Maggie's other nipple and teased it. She twisted and tugged on it until Maggie cried out as she reached her first climax.

"You're amazing," Maggie said.

"I'm just getting started."

"Oh, my."

Jean continued to tease Maggie's nipples until she came again. She continued to suck on one while she slid her hand between Maggie's legs. She found her wet and ready for her.

"You feel so good," Jean said.

"So do you."

Jean stroked Maggie's swollen clit.

"You're so ready for me."

"That's an understatement."

Jean continued to stroke her until Maggie cried out again.

"You're killing me," Maggie said.

"But what a way to go, yes?"

Maggie spread her legs wider to allow Jean greater access. Jean dipped her fingers inside, then dragged her juices all over her. She plunged her fingers deeper and deeper, massaging the satin walls and feeling them close around her.

She moved her mouth to Maggie's clit and drew it between her lips. She flicked her tongue over and under it. Maggie only lasted a few minutes before she screamed again.

"I can't take any more," she said.

"You sure? Because I'm just getting warmed up."

"I'm sure. I can't."

About the Author

MJ Williamz was raised on California's central coast, which she left at age seventeen to pursue an education. She graduated from Chico State, and it was in Chico that she rediscovered her love of writing. It wasn't until she moved to Portland, however, that her writing really took off, with the publication of her first short story in 2003. She hasn't looked back.

MJ is the author of six books, including the award-winning *Initiation by Desire*. She has also had over thirty short stories published, most of them erotica with a few romances and a few horrors thrown in for good measure.

MJ now lives in Houston with her wife and son.

Visit MJ's website at mjwilliamz.com or friend her on Facebook or follow her on Twitter at @MJ_Williamz.

Books Available From Bold Strokes Books

Making a Comeback by Julie Blair. Music and love take center stage when jazz pianist Liz Randall tries to make a comeback with the help of her reclusive, blind neighbor, Jac Winters. (978-1-62639-357-8)

Soul Unique by Gun Brooke. Self-proclaimed cynic Greer Landon falls for Hayden Rowe's paintings and the young woman shortly after, but will Hayden, who lives with Asperger syndrome, trust her and reciprocate her feelings? (978-1-62639-358-5)

The Price of Honor by Radclyffe. Honor and duty are not always black and white—and when self-styled patriots take up arms against the government, the price of honor may be a life. (978-1-62639-359-2)

Mounting Evidence by Karis Walsh. Lieutenant Abigail Hargrove and her mounted police unit need to solve a murder and protect wetland biologist Kira Lovell during the Washington State Fair. (978-1-62639-343-1)

Threads of the Heart by Jeannie Levig. Maggie and Addison Rae-McInnis share a love and a life, but are the threads that bind them together strong enough to withstand Addison's restlessness and the seductive Victoria Fontaine? (978-1-62639-410-0)

Sheltered Love by MJ Williamz. Boone Fairway and Grey Dawson—two women touched by abuse—overcome their pasts to find happiness in each other. (978-1-62639-362-2)

Searching for Celia by Elizabeth Ridley. As American spy novelist Dayle Salvesen investigates the mysterious disappearance of her ex-lover, Celia, in London, she begins questioning how well she knew Celia—and how well she knows herself. (978-1-62639-356-1).

Hardwired by C.P. Rowlands. Award-winning teacher Clary Stone and Leefe Ellis, manager of the homeless shelter for small children, stand together in a part of Clary's hometown that she never knew existed. (978-1-62639-351-6)

The Muse by Meghan O'Brien. Erotica author Kate McMannis struggles with writer's block until a gorgeous muse entices her into a world of fantasy sex and inadvertent romance. (978-1-62639-223-6)

No Good Reason by Cari Hunter. A violent kidnapping in a Peak District village pushes Detective Sanne Jensen and lifelong friend Dr. Meg Fielding closer, just as it threatens to tear everything apart. (978-1-62639-352-3)

Romance by the Book by Jo Victor. If Cam didn't keep disrupting her life, maybe Alex could uncover the secret of a century-old love story, and solve the greatest mystery of all—her own heart. (978-1-62639-353-0)

Death's Doorway by Crin Claxton. Helping the dead can be deadly: Tony may be listening to the dead, but she needs to learn to listen to the living. (978-1-62639-354-7)

The 45th Parallel by Lisa Girolami. Burying her mother isn't the worst thing that can happen to Val Montague when she returns to the woodsy but peculiar town of Hemlock, Oregon. (978-1-62639-342-4)

A Royal Romance by Jenny Frame. In a country where class still divides, can love topple the last social taboo and allow Queen Georgina and Beatrice Elliot, a working-class girl, their happy ever after? (978-1-62639-360-8)

Bouncing by Jaime Maddox. Basketball coach Alex Dalton has been bouncing from woman to woman because no one ever held her interest, until she meets her new assistant, Britain Dodge. (978-1-62639-344-8)

Same Time Next Week by Emily Smith. A chance encounter between Alex Harris and the beautiful Michelle Masters leads to a whirlwind friendship and causes Alex to question everything she's ever known—including her own marriage. (978-1-62639-345-5)

All Things Rise by Missouri Vaun. Cole rescues a striking pilot who crash-lands near her family's farm, setting in motion a chain of events that will forever alter the course of her life. (978-1-62639-346-2)

Riding Passion by D. Jackson Leigh. Mount up for the ride through a sizzling anthology of chance encounters, buried desires, romantic surprises, and blazing passion. (978-1-62639-349-3)

Love's Bounty by Yolanda Wallace. Lobster boat captain Jake Myers stopped living the day she cheated death, but meeting greenhorn Shy Silva stirs her back to life. (978-1-62639334-9)

Just Three Words by Melissa Brayden. Sometimes the one you want is the one you least suspect…Accountant Samantha Ennis has her ordered life disrupted when heartbreaker Hunter Blair moves into her trendy Soho loft. (978-1-62639-335-6)

Lay Down the Law by Carsen Taite. Attorney Peyton Davis returns to her Texas roots to take on big oil and the Mexican Mafia, but will her investigation thwart her chance at true love? (978-1-62639-336-3)

Playing in Shadow by Lesley Davis. Survivor's guilt threatens to keep Bryce trapped in her nightmare world unless Scarlet's love can pull her out of the darkness back into the light. (978-1-62639-337-0)

Soul Selecta by Gill McKnight. Soul mates are hell to work with. (978-1-62639-338-7)

Shadow Hunt by L.L. Raand. With young to raise and her Pack under attack, Sylvan, Alpha of the wolf Weres, takes on her greatest challenge when she determines to uncover the faceless enemies known as the Shadow Lords. A Midnight Hunters novel. (978-1-62639-326-4)

Heart of the Game by Rachel Spangler. A baseball writer falls for a single mom, but can she ever love anything as much as she loves the game? (978-1-62639-327-1)

Prayer of the Handmaiden by Merry Shannon. Celibate priestess Kadrian must defend the kingdom of Ithyria from a dangerous enemy and ultimately choose between her duty to the Goddess and the love of her childhood sweetheart, Erinda. (978-1-62639-329-5)

The Witch of Stalingrad by Justine Saracen. A Soviet "night witch" pilot and American journalist meet on the Eastern Front in WWII and struggle through carnage, conflicting politics, and the deadly Russian winter. (978-1-62639-330-1)